LITTLE BLUE MARBLE
2020

GREENER FUTURES

EDITED BY KATRINA ARCHER

ganache
media

A Ganache Media Book

Vancouver

2020 Ganache Media Print edition

Cover design by Katrina Archer

www.ganachemedia.com

littlebluemarble.ca

LITTLE BLUE MARBLE 2020

2020

GREENER FUTURES

For everyone coping with this year as best they can

CONTENTS

INTRODUCTION

WELCOME to the collected stories and poems of *Little Blue Marble* from 2020. All of these stories are available for free online because *Little Blue Marble*'s mission is to educate and inspire, not to make a profit. We thank you, however, because your purchase of this anthology will help us bring you more great stories about the climate crisis, and keep our mission on track.

2020 has been a rough year for many, as the coronavirus pandemic becomes possibly the first very visible global consequence of the climate crisis. While there is no evidence COVID-19 is a direct result of climate change, many scientists feel that given the ongoing loss of wildlife habitat, it is an inevitability that this is not the last time we shall be impacted as a species by a new virus. The World Health Organization states that climate change "undermines environmental determinants of health, and places additional stress on health systems. More generally, most emerging infectious diseases, and almost all recent pandemics, originate in wildlife, and there is evidence that increasing human pressure on the natural environment may drive disease emergence."[1]

The stories in *Little Blue Marble 2020* touch only glancingly if at all on our current pandemic world, but one theme is strong throughout: people struggling with moral decisions as a result of humanity's influence on the environment. As the consequences of our effect on the planet become more severe and extreme, it becomes imperative that we as a species unite around a new ethical framework, one that takes the health of our entire biosphere into account.

It's difficult to prioritize climate action in the middle of a different kind of global emergency, one that continues to take lives and ruin livelihoods. Thank you once again for devoting a small part of your attention this year to *Little Blue Marble*.

Be well.

— *Katrina Archer, Publisher & Editor,* Little Blue Marble

---

1. https://www.who.int/news-room/q-a-detail/coronavirus-disease-covid-19-climate-change

QUEEN OF THE MAY

F. E. Clark

SHE wears a fox's face—sly, and only dripping a little blood down the sides of its muzzle—as she emerges into the allotments from between gorse bushes where the path used to run. In a potting shed, brewing tea, a gardener sets out another cup thinking his friend's arrived. If she'd asked he'd have told her she was too early, that there were frosts to come, but she just picks a flower to wear in her hair, and keeps moving, heading for the city centre. Roadkill face, arms twined with ghost orchids, desiccated bees' nest and the flower in her hair. A train of fragrant blossoms, red, orange, pink, and purple, falls in her wake.

High scents of blood, fox, and horse steam from her as she moves through the dawn landscape. She's walking her ancient byway, as she has every year for millennia at the head of her parade, but now she walks alone. She looks to the sky for the flight of swallows that used to wheel in formation above her as she went, but they've not made it back yet.

Soon she leaves the grass behind and her hooves echo on pavements and tarmac. She walks like a prancing horse, her sleek skin shining. Cars and lorries thunder past. She sets her own pace, walking a line between the lanes of vehicles. A child on a halted bus jabs his chubby finger at the steamed up window, but his mother does not see the translucent wings folded at the shoulder blades of the vision that walks alongside them. The child decides that he too will have wings one day.

Reaching the main street she begins a slow-motion stepping—stopping and freezing with every leg raise, amid the blaring car horns and shouts of angry commuters. She stops dead centre in the road where the Maypole once stood, aiming a quick backward kick with the sharp edge of her hoof at a taxi that edges too close. The traffic stills about her. Her once-white dress hangs in tatters. She turns her magnificent, horrific head from side to side—taking in the territory. Recent past forgotten, she looks for the gathering, the celebration of Spring and the coming Summer, but can see only exhaust fumes, greed, and rage.

City grit sticks to her front teeth. She stumbles, attempts to begin her speech but her throat is full of sores and all that comes out is a rising gale that throws her plastic-threaded mane up high, dislodging the flower and the dead bees—bringing tears to her eyes. Her train of blossoms swirls. She places her hands on her rounded belly, rights herself. A

4

woman on her way home from her cleaning job sees the swelling belly and remembers her first pregnancy.

The city pauses, though most cannot see why and imagine an incident, a bomb, a shooting. Early April—she's too early this year for her day. Her axis tilted and accelerated, belly full, blossom cast to the winds and wilting as it falls. But here she is, May Day or not—and the city waits.

In a coffee shop, the clatter and chatter stop, a barista pauses midfroth to look out. A cyclist sees the power of the wind and remembers a free-wheeling fresh-air ride down the roadside of a loch. Gulls on granite ledges of the old buildings quieten and cock their heads, as if hearing the beat of an old familiar drum. High above street level, in a shiny office block, a besuited crowd gathers at a window. They hold take-away coffee cups and murmur of a disturbance, a protest, an accident, but it's too far to see what's going on, and the windows don't open so they hear nothing.

She raises the fox's face, baring her true face beneath. The blood smearing her cheeks does not hide her broken, raw beauty. A dolphin swims in the blue of her left eye—a microchip is mired in her left, golden pollen sits on her eyelashes. The city still around her, the still point in her heart mostly intact, fox from the road, great auk feather, forgotten flowers, horse conjured by a wish—she's a chimera for the end of times.

Her tears flood the city, as the gale rises. She does not know what is growing in her belly or if she will return next year, and her silent scream is never-ending. The spoilt blossom is still falling when, with flick of her tail, she's gone.

ABOUT THE AUTHOR

F. E. Clark lives in Scotland. She writes, paints, and takes photographs—inspired by nature in all its forms. A Pushcart, Best of the Net, Best Small Fictions, and Best Microfictions nominee, her poetry, flash fiction, and short stories can be found in anthologies and literary magazines. This story was inspired by folklore and climate change.

THE DESERT IN ME

Priya Chand

I was going to be a desert.

They'd designed this recliner for conductivity, not comfort. I lay down, feeling cold alloy through my shift because it was either "rehabilitation" or relocation.

"Where did they assign you for Environment Week?" the guard asked.

"I don't remember." It was twenty years ago. You turn eighteen, and they ship you off to be part of the landscape, literally, for an entire week. Happy goddamn birthday.

"Hmph." Cold gel on my temple. "It's important to remember how our actions change the planet, you know. One month will do you good." The guard's sincerity made me want to scream.

The electrodes connected.

I was drying out from the inside. The thought of

ungluing my lips, letting air corrode my throat, was too much. So I waited and let it happen and then I blinked.

I was miles of dust crisscrossed with buried riverbeds. We'd drained the aquifers, so there were no oases in me. Nothing at all, except red fire ants and the heat. My surface was baking.

No, I wouldn't let go yet. My *skin* cracked open, insects drifted between my pores. I was supposed to put this miserable ecosystem before myself? Screw that. I'd take all the long hot showers I wanted. My thoughts went in tight, angry circles. I lost count of the days. One after another, all the same, trying to change me.

And then, one cool silent night, the air hinted at moisture. Oh god. I had come to terms with my dryness by forgetting wet.

I moaned.

"Are you OK?"

No, I'm not OK, I'm a desert. But I couldn't say that to a person who was an air current flecked with sea salt. "I'm holding up."

"Happy birthday!"

I chose not to tell my new friend I was a thirty-eight-year-old criminal. "Thank you."

Their winds ruffled my expanse, which was unperturbed by tiny skulls and the remnants of saguaro. Some said that murderers and rapists were left to wallow there forever. But I hadn't heard any voices from them, so maybe not.

"How are you enjoying your first environmental

dissociation?"

I wanted to strangle the neighbour who reported my busted meter. "Fine," I said.

"I love it." Their voice caught every time the winds shifted, which was constantly. I-ha-love-ha-it-ha. Playacting. "You don't get a choice when it's your first, but if you work hard, you can be the wind. I save up, buy a week, rinse and repeat."

"Sounds nice."

"It is magnificent. I hope you try it."

If I had the credits, I'd take hour-long showers and dump my trash in the landfill just because I could.

"I don't know," I said.

"You need to embrace it."

I said nothing. Let the wind think that, like the desert, I was an insect-riddled corpse.

"Focus on where my winds touch you, desert. I'm picking up sand, following the heat, I drift and roll. What do you feel?"

A caress. "Sand moving." Patterns and new patterns across my surface like fingers on skin. Winds rearranged my rolling curves. My consciousness flirted with a crack in the soil where the salt fell in, filling me, and then moved to a point where sand and wind formed words in a language that bloomed through my whole body. Through the desert.

I remembered tasting chocolate when I was sixteen, the summer my friends and I lifted a whole shipment for ourselves. Tasting and then coming back to it day after day, at our leisure, until it ran out, leaving my life once again as empty and bland as the desert.

But now, I experienced details I'd never noticed, the way my dips and rises shaped the flow of the current passing through me, the desert.

The wind shifted. "Oh, I'm going back towards the sea. Until tomorrow, I hope."

"Bye," I said.

The sun rose. I didn't need eyes to feel ants scurrying from their mounds, or the blossoming heat. As the desert spilled into my consciousness, I baked and froze with all of myself.

It was torture. It was what we had done to nature. I had thought my choices could be self-contained, that I was an island. The biggest lie of all.

In a thousand years, the rivers would flow, filling the aquifers, restoring whatever life found its way back here. And this desert would bloom.

I wouldn't see it, but I would be part of it. I would make sure of that.

ABOUT THE AUTHOR

Priya Chand grew up in San Diego and now resides in the vicinity of Chicago. She has previously been published in *Clarkesworld*, *Nature Futures*, and *Analog SF*, among others. Her interest in ecosystems stems from a background in biology and a love of marine life. When she's not reading, writing, or eating, she enjoys swimming, martial arts, and naps.

THE WOLF BOYS OF WIDE RIVER COUNTY

Eileen Gunnell Lee

New year, new rations, same drought. The Wide River still a dust bowl between the public house and homes to the south, the farms beyond. Despite the heat, people trickled in to pick up their water—even the outsiders, the temp workers here for the new development. They needed to drink too, I supposed.

The mayor lined up with everyone else during the after-dinner rush, looking less polished than usual. The broad green sheaths of her hair were flat, her skin shining with sweat. She leaned toward me and whispered as I lifted her water ration to the bar top. Her voice like wind through leaves sent shivers to the ends of me. She never talked like that, not when she was campaigning anyway. She said, "The Wolf Boys are coming, Raoula. I have it on good authority."

"You want me to change the locks and send 'em away?" We both laughed. But there was something dark as dirt behind her eyes even as her men collected the water and ushered her away.

• • •

The Wolf Boy must have killed his bike's engine and coasted into town. A Wolf Boy never padded into town like an animal with a secret. With Wolf Boys, it was all whooping and howling, screaming and snarling. Except for Rush, when he came for me. It was past 3 a.m. when he jimmied the lock, having refused my offer of a key as something too forward. Too conventional. Too permanent. He'd had a lot to say then, after our first night together, about the optics of a Wolf Boy having a key to an apartment belonging to the dyke fox at the public house. He'd insisted on this charade and I'd let him keep it. There was so little comfort in this world for tender souls.

But now I was dressed and sitting with my gun in my lap. As he crested the top step, it was primed and pointed. A girl couldn't be too careful. When I confirmed it was Rush, though, I tucked the gun into my bedside drawer and retrieved what I knew he was here for. The leather straps were soft and cool on my fingertips, the bare skin of my thighs.

He shook his head even as he pulled off his shirt, revealing raised hackles all the way from nape to ass crack. "Raoula, I have to tell you something."

Rush's body was a reed primed to the currents of feeling.

Even the thick fur that covered his shoulders, the backs of his arms, rippled and flicked in response to the smallest stimuli. I couldn't help but blow a hot breath over his back and watch the dance of Rush's anxiety in the gradient waves of his hair.

"After," I growled. And he did tell me after, when he was pooled and panting in my lap, and my hips were still aching with the effort.

"It's the mayor," Rush said. "She called us down. She has a job for us. It's messy. You're not gonna like it."

After Rush left, I hauled all the whiskey I had up to the bar. The Wolf Boys could be particular—but not that particular. One case of Maker's Mark and two of Jack. If the Wolf Boys were here for a job, we were going to need it.

• • •

Rush was at the bar, weight on his elbows as he perched at the edge of his seat like he was nursing hurt. I mixed a gimlet, feeling the sting of the lime on my fingers, and slid it down to him, undecided if it was an apology or a provocation. But before we could get into it, a Wolf Girl I'd not seen before pushed up to the bar, turned her jaw to me and yawned, long tongue lolling.

On closer inspection, maybe not a girl. Or a wolf. It was hard to tell these days, with everyone mixing their own genetic cocktails—girls, boys, enbies, wolves, foxes, martins, snakes, trees. I didn't give a fuck. If you ran with the wolves you were good in my eyes.

My thing for the mayor was an aberration in that regard.

But I'd had my eye on this willow-splice for a while, ever since she was not much more than a sapling on town council. I'd always liked soft things—and Rush was evidence of that. But he was a soft thing that others mistook for hard, him being a Wolf Boy and all. The mayor, though, she was a different kind of creature and this business with the wolves had already gone some way to confirm it. The way she hedged around what needed to be done, carefully weighing impacts before setting a plan in motion—the way she wore that consideration in the bend of her body—told me what I needed to know about the shape of her heartwood.

Turns out, it was the mayor that the young wolfling was eyeballing. Together we watched her gather her long limbs, shaking like an aspen as she moved to the back room with the biggest Wolf Boys. I counted the minutes in poured drinks and glasses washed and dried, but the mayor did not emerge until near closing. Even then she appeared well after the Wolf Boys had gathered up their ranks and screamed into the hills.

That night, the first of the outsiders from the developer's camp went missing.

• • •

I was tacking the week's new posters to the community board when the mayor swept past me, her leaves brushing the bare skin on the backs of my arms. She didn't turn to look at the faces of the missing—each of them with a wide, vacant gaze, some with horns or antlers unfiled. They were pictures taken from the developer's employee identification database, the stark lighting emphasizing a herbivore's backwards glance, as if each of the missing knew upon signing up for the job that they would become targets. That they were already prey. The mayor, though, she held her gaze straight as she pulled up to the end of the bar. But by the time I got her a glass, she was weeping.

I poured golden Solera deep and watched as she gulped it down and pushed her glass back to me. She was so beautiful, even as she trembled with sorrow. Her knotted skin was a dark grey-green. Black where her tears fell.

"Remember that experiment they did in Lamar Valley?" she asked, touching her glass to her lips and putting it down again without drinking. "The reintroduction of Mackenzie Valley wolves? How it produced a chain of effects that the scientists hadn't anticipated? The predators controlled the grazers, which allowed for vegetation to grow, which then brought the waters back to the land?" Her words were slurred, even as she breathed through the burn of her third drink.

I held my tongue, the whiskey in one hand and my hope gripped in the other.

"We have too many grazers. Too many who will take a bite out of anyone and anything they can. I had to call them, Raoula. The wolves. You understand, don't you?"

I nodded.

"I didn't think it would be so hard. You understand that, don't you, Raoula? I didn't think *I* would have to be so hard. Please, give me another drink and take me upstairs. Like you do with your Wolf Boy."

With my heart choking me, I closed my eyes. Shook my head. Swallowed. "Next time, Willa. If you still want it."

• • •

I dream of Willa in my bed a year later. My tongue in the crooks of her. Her rough skin scraping me raw. I dream of her even though she sends her men to pick up her orders. Even though she walks by without even looking at her own reflection in the pub window.

A year later, after the signs on the community board have faded, after the Wolf Boys have roared their return to the hills, I still dream of Willa. I dream that she will come to me, that she will lay down her grief, give up her shame, and say "Raoula, I did what I had to do, and look what's come of it!" I dream that her leafy crown will shake with laughter as she says, "Of course, I did it for myself. For my people, the trees. But all of you will prosper too." These dreams stay with me. They have made a home inside me: cool, verdant, growing. Growing.

My dream Willa is still with me when I come downstairs and wade through river water three feet deep, the power of it having collapsed the shelf behind the bar some weeks ago now. In the current, bottles bob about like they have urgent messages to deliver. Broken glass glints beneath clear eddies. I scoop some of the water—impossibly cool and clean—into a glass and drink.

ABOUT THE AUTHOR

Eileen Gunnell Lee is a writer, educator, a recent PhD in literature, and a general logophile. She has stories published in or forthcoming from *Nightmare Magazine, Escape Pod, Selene Quarterly, Fusion Fragment*, and others. As Selena Middleton, she is Publisher and Editor-in-Chief at Stelliform Press, where she champions a new wave of climate fiction that considers relations of all kinds as ecology. Living halfway up the Niagara Escarpment in Hamilton, Ontario, she regularly meets deer, foxes, coyotes, and cloaked riders on horseback.

GREEN-UP ON AISLE 13

Sarina Dorie

A wave of pollution rolled into the Bureau of Indian Affairs. I held my breath, fighting the urge to cough against the caustic air. A bundled-up man pushed through the doors, bringing with him the reek of petrol and a bluster of cold from the arctic temperatures outside.

I leapt to attention behind the counter, pushing the button of the holo projector I'd put in standby mode to conserve energy. The stark room around me became lit with a glow of golden light, the walls now adorned with blue skies and panoramic vistas of ancient pueblo ruins and desert landscapes. The counter transformed into the crumbling rock wall of a building. The visitor stepped forward and the red soil beneath his feet shifted toward him as though he was walking through the virtual scene of Chaco Canyon—or what Chaco Canyon had looked like based on photographs a hundred years ago.

Before the man had even removed the mask that made breathing outdoors in the pollution possible, he began to speak, his voice muffled. "Julie Bluehorse, did you hear about the petroglyphs? Someone vandalized them in the middle of the night."

I recognized the cadence of John Longhorn's voice. I swallowed. "Yes, I've heard."

Someone had blasted at the cliff just outside the city. Whether the artifacts had been destroyed or stolen, the tribe no longer had them. One more piece of our past was gone.

Longhorn removed two pairs of gloves and set them on the façade of stone bricks that was the counter. He pulled back his hood before yanking off his breathing mask. His dark eyes squinted at me from within a face mapped with wrinkles. "Well, have they caught the bastards yet?"

"No," I said, wishing my words carried good news.

He pointed an arthritic finger at me. "Damn it, you need to do something about this."

"Why come to me and not Sheriff Redfeather?" I asked.

John Longhorn clenched his breathing mask in his wrinkled hands so tightly his fingers blanched. "You know why. What's he going to do? Arrest that son of his and his no-good friends?"

"You have no proof. How do you expect me to help?" I was just as disgusted as him. Three counts of vandalism and no proof yet to convict those everyone knew to be at fault.

The old man stared into my eyes, the intensity of his gaze

piercing me to my core as he leaned over the counter. "We must protect the tribe's history and show respect for the artifacts we have left. The little we have left." The conviction in his voice faded, making him sound softer and frailer. It sickened my stomach hearing the despair in Longhorn's voice. It sickened my heart knowing a little more of our culture was lost.

I shifted my gaze to the two-by-two-foot window to the side of the counter that overlooked our reality: an eyesore of high-rise vistas, flashy casinos, and the clashing electric lights of the overpopulated city. "I can't help you. Go down to the twenty-third floor to the police station."

John Longhorn turned away in disgust, his gaze sweeping over the wall projections of what New Mexico once looked like before being covered with nine feet of ice. "You ain't any better than the sheriff."

I turned off the projection, returning the office to its banal state. I hated the system I was part of, powerless to aid those who truly needed it.

• • •

In the supermarket, I tucked my baseball cap lower down on my forehead as John Longhorn's words echoed in my head. He was right. I'd been catering to the sheriff, the mayor, the tourists, to everyone who had power.

The aroma of ponderosa pines mingling with dusty desert sand and thunderstorms contrasted sharply with the fluorescent lights and artificial air of the grocery store. I peeled back the mask that made breathing outside in the twenty-second-century pollution possible. The out-of-place scent of nature reminded me of my childhood, when trees stood in places other than heated reserves protected by biodomes. Perhaps it was simply an air freshener, but it didn't smell like artificial perfumes.

The swarm of white men and women in the temperature-regulated grocery store towered over my diminutive frame as I quickly shoved groceries into my cart.

"Hello, sister," a white-as-bread, Native American wannabe said with his long tawny hair worn down. From his excessive silver and turquoise jewelry I suspected he was a tourist.

I said nothing, in no mood to pretend to be thrilled other cultures thought they were adopting my people's traditions when we had just lost a big piece of our history.

I hurried to the checkout line with the meagre selection of groceries I could afford on my salary. My salt-and-pepper bun hidden under my cap and eyes masked behind sun goggles, I avoided eye contact with gaping tourists who had come to the arctic temperatures of New Mexico to see the last of the real Native Americans. I tapped my tundra boot with impatience, ready to be out of the swamped market and finally rest after a long day at work.

I had taken the job thinking I might be able to help people, to help my people. Yet each day ended with more frustrations than I had begun with.

The perfume of wet wood and clean rain caught my attention. The woman in line in front of me had the kind of long black hair that made the tourists stare. She placed items from her basket onto the checkout stand. Pricey imported items: real maple syrup, a giant bag of organic fertilizer, dried dates, jerky made from meat and not soy protein. I watched the intricate pattern sewn into her long brown sleeve undulate as she moved. She set down more maple.

I chuckled. "Wow, someone really likes—"

She turned to look at me, a wicked grin on her skeletal face. Well, it wasn't really skeletal, but the way the intersecting twigs, layers of moss, and lichen came together to make up her features gave her a skeletal look.

I tensed, thinking of Coyote and other tricksters. I reminded myself she wasn't here to harm me. Most likely she was what my grandmother from Rhode Island called a chepi, a kind of nature spirit. I glanced at the people around me to see if anyone saw what I saw. A young man in the next checkout line over winked at her, a cocky grin on his face. His friend elbowed him in the ribs, leering. I immediately recognized the second youth as the sheriff's son.

Wishing to stare anywhere but at them, I glanced at the security mirror on the ceiling. The chepi looked like an ordinary woman. Or as ordinary as an aging, voluptuous woman in tight jeans and a low-cut shirt could.

She set two more maple syrups on the belt and then the two canvas bags. Written on one of them were the words: "Save a tree, save a life." She counted out a pile of green leaves and placed brown clumps of dirt on top, her eyes never leaving the face of the robotic cashier.

I knew what she was trying to do. She was trying to trick him with magic. I'd seen it before. Had he been a real person, the cashier would get in trouble for his till coming up short later, just as my brother once did in my parents' shop. But this was a computer-automated checkout stand, and the chepi's magic surely couldn't work on a machine, could it? She would get caught trying to "steal." And then what would happen to her?

On the other hand, the chepi would have no way to pay for what she could no longer find in her natural habitat. Frustration at the lack of solution rose up in my chest.

This was the first time I'd seen one of the chepi in the city. When I was a child, I used to see them come into my parents' feed store on the reservation—back when there were reservations. They'd marauded in, dressed as farmers and Native Americans as they came in to buy ammonium nitrate. Only I noticed the flashes of twiggy patchwork in the place of skin, masks of leaves woven into moss—simultaneously beautiful and frightening. I soon learned to keep my mouth shut, as confessions of what I'd seen resulted in a whack on the backside of the head from my parents. I learned to dislike seeing these tricksters. With them always came trouble.

When I was eight, I threw a rock at one of them as they walked out of the store.

"Not everyone can see with eyes like yours," my grandmother said. "The tribes here in New Mexico call them tricksters, but the Narragansett call them chepi. Do not spite them for your ability to see their true nature. They have been pushed off their land like us and no longer fit into this world. There are few left, and fewer still to believe in them."

She told me stories of the Narragansett tribes and how the chepi used to come to them, in visions to warn us of dangers or remind us of their existence. "They take because we no longer give to them," she said. "It never hurts to sacrifice fertilizer or seeds to the spirits if that's what they desire. There was a time when they once destroyed our enemies and avenged injustice for us."

Looking out at the dry, desolate reservation covered in frost despite the summer temperatures, I had crossed my arms, parroting words I had heard my parents say in the past. "Yeah, and we can see how well that worked."

I didn't have the heart for this, I told myself then. Using magic, or whatever this ability was, didn't fit into this modern age of depleted ozone and climate change any more than the chepi did.

I resented my abilities. When I grew old enough to take over the till, I refused to accept payment from the chepi and turned them away when they tried to buy from us. Those were the days back before the government banned unlicensed farmers from buying ammonium nitrate. They said they didn't want terrorists to get their hands on it. Locals said it was to keep the poor man poorer.

I now wondered if the government knew about the nature spirits and meant to spite them, to crush them out of existence so there would be one less minority to share the land with. Their situation wasn't the kind of thing one person could fix. Especially not someone like me.

Why did I see them? And why now of all times? What would Grandmother say about this: that it was a warning, or a reminder?

The chepi glanced over her shoulder at me, her twiggy smile uneasy as if she was wondering if I would give her away. I noticed the foil gum wrapper twisted around her finger. A bottle cap was lodged in between the lacework of juniper and dried sagebrush at her wrist. Hanging from a piece of electrical wire at her neck was a fragment of rumpled potato-chip bag. Instead of wearing precious metals and jewels given by my people as offerings, she wore garbage. Was this the best a nature spirit could do for gifts in an age that had cast the natural world aside?

I looked away, feeling guilty as I remembered how I had once treated her people. The metal arm of the robot cashier separated the leaves from the clumps of dirt. The overly cheery mechanized voice announced. "This currency is not acceptable. An attendant will be with you shortly."

The chepi glanced over her shoulder, eyes wide with panic. She scooped up her groceries in her arms, looking like she was about to bolt. Were chepi reduced to stealing because no one made them offerings these days?

I couldn't stand it anymore. "No, stop," I said.

I swept the leaves and dirt from the robotic hands.

"You don't need to pay," I told her firmly. "I will help you."

Her eyebrows rose. I nodded, making up my mind. I

doubted it could atone for my years of disrespect and neglect, but it was a start.

I wrote a cheque, hesitating as I calculated how much the chepi's bill would cost in addition to my own. It was a stretch for my savings, especially with all her pricey, organic items. But then, I supposed it wouldn't be a true sacrifice if it was easy. The chepi needed real offerings. They needed me and others like me to believe in them again. I might have denied what I'd seen with my own eyes before, but that didn't mean I couldn't make up for lost time.

The chepi walked off with her canvas bag of groceries, a triumphant smile on her face. The bottle cap lodged in her wrist fell out and rolled on the floor. It hit the boot of the sheriff's son. He craned his neck to get a better view of her rear. As the chepi walked past, the bottom of his backpack tore, and a large chunk of bubble-wrapped sandstone spilled out onto the floor.

"Isn't that the missing petroglyph?" someone in the store shouted.

The chepi glanced over her shoulder at me and winked. Curling around the decaying twigs of her face was a green leaf, fresh and vibrant with life.

ABOUT THE AUTHOR

Sarina Dorie has sold over 150 short stories to markets like *Analog, Daily Science Fiction, F & SF*, and *Orson Scott Card's IGMS*. Her stories and published novels have won humour contests and Romance Writer of America awards. She has about fifty books up on Amazon, including her bestselling series, *Womby's School for Wayward Witches*.

A few of her favourite things include: gluten-free brownies (not necessarily glutton-free), Star Trek, steampunk aesthetics, fairies, Severus Snape, Captain Jack Sparrow, and Mr. Darcy.

You can find info about her short stories and novels on her website: www.sarinadorie.com.

SEEING CLEARLY

Marie Vibbert

THE water in the tank that circled the Mermaid Dining Room had gotten brackish and thick. Edwidge crawled onto a plasticine rock inside the tank. Her turbine sputtered and whined as it broke into the air. Papery algae slid under her silicone-coated fingers. She had to get to the performance cave.

From the performance cave, when the doors to the dining room were open and the sun was out, it looked like the ocean was close enough to touch.

The doors were not open, but she still wanted to get to where she could confirm that.

Edwidge's tail had forty-seven rows of articulated scales made of titanium alloy and covered in a rainbow of glass enamel. The articulation allowed for a variety of realistic fishtail motions, but in truth a turbine engine in her pelvis propelled her through the water.

She swayed her tail as she moved, the jets of water passing through the spaces between articulations. The scales disrupted the flow, made it turbulent, and she used this for fine steering control as she swam in her ring around the dining room. Her durable plastic hair wafted behind her.

Her program was to engage diners who wanted engagement, waving, smiling, doing small tricks. She had many subroutines to understand and anticipate needs. In the cave, the widest area of the tank, she could perform flips and twists and catch glimpses of the glittering water, out there, beyond the corridor, where the diners came from.

She used to leap the archway; the tank was open on top and extended over the walking path. The leap was flashy and too distracting for some patrons, so she had only been allowed to do it one to three times a night, depending on crowd size. But the top of the archway dried out quickly. While the water was still high enough, she did one flip per evening. There were no longer any patrons to distract, but Edwidge felt better if she kept within ordered parameters.

The last human she'd seen had been an old woman who had asked her if she wanted to be shut off, because the woman didn't know how long it would be before the restaurant opened again. Edwidge shook her head because she'd rather swim, and that had been that.

It hadn't been the first large storm. The staff cleared the tables, stacked the chairs, and covered the far window. Everything tucked and covered and braced, snug and safe, and the doors closed last, like the clasp of a gift box. Then came the strange, lonely sounds, the hotel creaking and moaning through the night. Unlike the storms before, no one burst into the room after saying, "Back to work!"

No one came at all.

A pool of brackish water, thick with dead things, lay between her and the next rock. Alarms warned her of the risk of damage, of malfunction, but she snoozed them all and slid into the slime.

Her eyes, as long as they were clear, could emit a beam of concentrated, coherent light that killed algae. But the dead algae flaked off into the water and clogged the filters. At first, she cleaned anything and everything—everything but the fish and scuttling creatures in the tank—she wasn't to use her lasers on animals—but even with the snails and the little starfish robot, she couldn't keep up against the growth forever.

The fish had stopped moving, and then the little, scuttling things. That made her sad. She was designed to be interested in movement.

She snoozed the warnings about animal life and carefully cleaned a crab, but though it waved one claw weakly, it never moved again.

As the water lowered, she swam circles, wanting to use all of her tank while she had it. That was perhaps short-sighted. She paused atop the next ornamental rock: another slimy pool lay between her and the cave. Dried moss hung from the shallow depression of concrete like hair. Her own hair was thick with detritus and hung in unpredictable clumps. She had to shake her head to clear her vision.

All that struggle to be opposite the archway again, and the view remained unchanged: empty chairs and tables, closed doors.

Where had the diners gone? Where had the servers gone and the people with the brushes to tickle small particles of dirt from her scales?

She had to leave the tank or she would become another still, dry thing in it. Even the starfish robot had stopped moving. She felt her isotope cell, constant in her chest. She would function a century yet, and she felt every second ahead of her. She was not designed to leave the tank. But she had spent so long putting off action because she could try to clean the tank, and then she put off action because she could pace the tank, and now ... there was nothing more she could do.

Here, at least, the tank, designed to be just wide enough for her hips, was narrowed by the concrete stalactites. She put one hand on the cave and one on the tank glass and lifted herself. With the pressure of her arms on opposite surfaces, she could crawl upward. Her hair persistently dropped into her view. She let it stay. She knew the shape of the space. Slapping the walls alternately with her tail, she reached the top and clung there. She calculated trajectory. She ignored a warning against entering an area where she could harm or be harmed by patrons. She calculated again and tumbled like a flounder to the floor.

A bristly fabric with seashells and bubbles drawn on it covered the floor. Her scales caught on this and she twitched to move forward. She wasn't sure where she was going, but it made sense to head to the doors.

Chips of enamel fell from her scales. She varied her motions to even out the wear and damage.

The doors did not budge as she pushed them. She looked up, above her at the brass curved handles she had seen staff clutch and turn. She reached. Her fingers grazed wood, inches below. She was not made for this. She was made to swim in the tank. She was made to perform tricks.

She executed a flip. Her turbine whined uselessly. Her tail slapped the floor. She flew upward and missed the handle on the way down. The silicone skin split on her left elbow when she hit the floor. Alerts swam across her vision. She had to take a moment and snooze them. She tried again.

The doors swung open as she hung from the handle.

She'd never seen this place, a corridor along the front of the hotel, one wall a long window, broken in places. Chaise lounges faced it, some folded neatly, others tumbled. In both directions the window and the chairs marched into the distance. One direction was slightly shorter. She turned that way. The floor—tile here—did not aid her with traction but also did not wear as badly on her silicone fingers. She pushed through pieces of scattered, broken window glass that sounded like her tail against the tiles. She reached the first great hole in the wall.

The ocean flowed into archways and square gaps in the

hotel below, curling foam around pillars as the waves sucked in and out. The water was farther than the floor had been from the top of her tank. Edwidge wasn't sure she could survive the drop.

Crawling onward, she passed an open storage closet, empty, shelves cleared of all but a few canisters. She felt a hot resentment. For these things, someone had come.

The corridor ended in stairs. Edwidge rolled sideways, one step at a time. Around her the hotel lobby opened, with its curving desk designed to look like a coral reef, and a statue that looked like Edwidge. Then more wide steps, white marble and red carpet covered in moss near the water that lapped four steps below.

A crystal chandelier dangled half into the water, dragging bits of plastic and seaweed. Rivulets of light reflected on the ceiling, let in with the ocean through the colonnade of destroyed windows.

Once she was in water, Edwidge could move easily again. The water was cloudy. Not as bad as the tank, but not as clear as the tank used to be. Small things with legs scuttled under overturned chairs and luggage racks. It was good to see their kind again.

The ocean was not rough in the hotel lobby; the break-wall formed by the front wall of the hotel muted the waves. Edwidge wriggled through the revolving door and felt the dirt wash from her inner workings, her turbine cutting water again at last.

This was so much more interesting than her tank. There

was movement everywhere! Swaying plants as tall as the ocean, fish darting together through a tangle of plastic tubes. Concrete gave way to sand, dotted only with signs urging to swim at your own risk when lifeguards were not on duty. Then the ocean floor dropped into so much open space.

A school of silver fish danced around her. Edwidge did her tricks—not because anyone was watching but because she wanted to.

And then—some time later—she saw a human! Her sensors picked up right away a shadow on the surface. She swam toward it and sure enough, a human was sitting astride a plank in the water. It was not how she was used to seeing them. She waved and the human fell off his plank.

She watched him swim under it and take hold of it. He stared at her. She did a twirl and a flip. He laughed and slapped his plank.

The next day more humans appeared, in boats and on planks and on soft round things that floated. It was fun, performing again, and this audience seemed more appreciative. They were darker than the restaurant patrons, with tangled hair and simple, rough clothing. Since there was no glass between them, she could hear their shouts of joy, and see the fine lines at the corners of their eyes.

It was lovely performing again, until the day the large white boat came, and they threw a net over her.

Edwidge didn't know what to make of that, but they drew her out of the water and onto the boat, and a man touched her face. "Look at you," he said. "From the old hotel. I can't believe you're still working." He looked more like the restaurant patrons, with a smart cap with an anchor on it like the seating hostess wore.

Edwidge had too many questions and no mechanism for vocal communication.

"Yes," he said. "I know. It was horrible, leaving you alone so long. But don't worry. We built a new hotel, see?" He pointed.

The boat had been moving along the shore. The old hotel barely stuck out from the water, other dilapidated buildings near it, but now instead of dominating the landward view, it slipped behind a rocky promontory. Where the man with the hostess cap pointed, a new copy of the hotel, larger and grander, rose over cobbled shacks of wood and tin.

"There's a nice tank waiting for you," the man said. "With a waterfall!"

Edwidge thought about returning to a tank. About a world slightly wider than her hips. She felt his hands squeezing her silicone into her arm-struts. He held her like he would never let her go. An alert popped up. *Stuck.* She wriggled her unsticking pattern and he laughed, hoisting her, other hands joining his.

The man said, "We're bringing it all back. One piece at a time."

Stuck, her alert blinked. She locked her gaze with him, and she used her cleaning laser to burn his eyes.

He screamed and let go, his companions gathering him into their arms. She threw herself over the side of the boat.

The humans might be foolish enough to keep doing the same things, but she wasn't.

ABOUT THE AUTHOR

Besides selling fifty-odd short stories, a dozen poems and a few comics, Marie Vibbert has been a medieval (SCA) squire, ridden 17% of the roller coasters in the United States, and has played O-line and D-line for the Cleveland Fusion women's tackle football team.

THE PINECONE LADY

Jo Miles

WE were suffering through the hottest, thirstiest, cruelest season yet when the Pinecone Lady came through town. I've heard a lot of theories about her since then, about who she was or *what* she was, but those theories are all missing the point. I only care what she did—because what she did meant everything.

In the town where I grew up, we didn't talk about summers and autumns anymore. There was just winter, spring, and fire season. Even at twelve years old, I knew that each fire season would be worse than the one before, and the green, easy summers before I was born existed only in my moms' stories. On the hottest, windiest afternoons, when they cut the power to prevent fires, we sat on the porch sipping water and listening to our hand-crank radio, waiting for alerts, watching for signs of smoke. Those seasons turned towns with names like Paradise into a real-world hell.

This wasn't one of the worst days, though. The fire risk was only high, not severe, so Mama let me ride my bike to Sequoia Park as long as I kept my phone and face mask with me. This park was no more than a bit of scrubby grass and a few surviving trees squeezed between two half-empty strip malls, across the street from a wilting field of sugar beets. Even the newest genetically engineered crops were struggling with this hot, dry weather, my moms said. Fortunately, with the calm winds today, the rotting-compost smell of the sugar refinery outside town didn't reach us.

I settled in to read a book under the biggest tree, a welcoming old oak, and that's where she found me.

"That's a nice tree you've got," the stranger said. She stopped her bike at the side of the road, one foot on the curb to keep her balance.

I stretched so the bark scratched my back. "Thanks, but it's not *my* tree. It's my friend, and it lets me sit here to keep it company."

I wasn't sure why I said that last part, because that sort of thing made most adults look at me funny, or chuckle as if I was joking, but she grinned like I'd said something extra clever. "Why do you think it lets you?"

"It's lonely, I think because it lost all its friends in the fire when I was little. So I think it likes having me around, even though I'm not a tree."

She leaned her bike against a parking meter and came over to squat beside me in the shade. She was young for a grownup, and pretty, with light brown skin and long black hair that fell in waves down her back, but the thing I noticed most was her eyes: rich brown one moment, then green as the oak's leaves the next. She looked at me and the tree like she saw things other people didn't.

"That's very wise of you," she said. "Not all kids know how to listen to trees, and almost everyone forgets by the time they're adults."

"But not you?" I asked, because she didn't seem to be teasing me.

"Not me. I think the very best thing we can do is be good friends to our trees. And you're right about this one. Did you know that trees in a forest talk to each other? Not in words, but in chemical signals through their roots. They take care of each other, warning each other about weather and insect attacks and whatever else could hurt them. But when they lose their families, like these trees have ... yes, I think they get lonely, in their own way."

"Who are you?" I asked. "You don't talk like a grownup."

"Thank you!" She laughed. "You've heard of Johnny Appleseed? Well, you can call me the Pinecone Lady."

"That's not a real name!" I said, but she only shrugged. "My name's Daphne. Where are you from?" She had an accent, like a familiar song I couldn't quite recognize.

"Oh, I'm from here, there, and everywhere. I go where I'm needed. Wherever we've lost too many trees. Do you know how trees are connected to our weather, and our climate?"

"In school, we learned that fossil fuels made the climate change, but that cutting down all the trees made it worse. Because of ..." My forehead wrinkled as I tried to remember. "Because of how they trap carbon dioxide."

"Good! You know all about this. You're exactly right. Trees are better at trapping carbon dioxide than any of the atmospheric scrubbers we've built. No human has figured out how to make something as wonderful as a tree. But cutting down trees pushed the climate over the edge, and I'm working to make it better."

"It's too late to make it better. It'll only get worse."

Everyone knew that. Every kid in my class had known it our whole lives: the world was on fire, and people gave up on putting it out a long time ago. We grew up waiting for it to cook us alive.

"What if it didn't have to?" She picked up a leaf from the ground, twirled the stem between her fingers. "Your friend here might like a say in the matter. What if we help it to help us?"

"The oak? How?"

She grinned at me. "Can I show you something magical, Daphne?"

The Pinecone Lady was a stranger, technically, but she didn't feel like one, and I really wanted very badly to know what she meant. I nodded hard.

She fetched a saddlebag from her bike and pulled out a handful of ... stuff. There were pinecones, and acorns, and walnuts in their shells, and other things I didn't recognize.

They all looked like seeds. "This spot used to be a forest, you know. A century ago, most of the trees got cut down and turned into farmland. Now half the farmland's been paved over, and most of the surviving trees have died or burned. But we can fix that. Let's see, what to start with? How about a sequoia?"

"They don't grow here."

"Not now, but they used to. Here, hold your hands." She held up a fist-sized pinecone, which she pried and twisted apart with her fingers. Seeds like tiny light-coloured coffee beans rained into my hands. They felt like they might float away, fragile and precious as gold. I cupped my hands around them and followed her to a spot of broken pavement at the edge of the strip mall.

"Are you *planting* them? They'll die here!"

"Nope, because we're going to help them." She cupped her hands around mine and blew on the seeds, and ... they glowed. Even in the hot, sweaty sun, the seeds glowed like fallen stars. "There. Now plant one," she whispered. "Give it some earth, and tell it to grow."

"Tell it? I can't ..."

"You talk to your friend, the oak tree, right?"

"That's different."

"It's more the same than you think. You talk to trees, Daphne, and you listen to them. This is no different. Here." She tucked one seed into a gaping crack in the pavement and hovered her hands over it, humming. "Help me," she murmured. "Tell it to grow, to be strong and brave. Tell it we need it. Picture a whole forest for it to join."

I squeezed my eyes shut, my free hand joining hers. I pictured the forest that used to live here, vast and shady and strong, a forest full of friends for my oak tree.

"A forest so vast it captures water and cools the ground and cleans the air. A forest big enough to wrap and cradle our whole planet, to nurture it and keep it safe ..."

The image filled my mind, and even the sun felt cooler for a minute. And when she took her hands away ...

There was a seedling. A tiny, delicate, perfect baby sequoia, stretching out its tiny baby branches covered in needles so fine they felt soft.

"Oh," I breathed. "How did you do that?"

"*We* did it," she said. "I figured out a long time ago that I could help trees grow, and I realized pretty quickly how important that was. Planting trees won't fix our world when it's so broken, but *unless* we bring back the trees, there's no hope for any other solution. Trees could get us moving in the right direction, I thought, so I've planted them everywhere I can: here in California, and in Brazil, Indonesia, Cameroon, Canada ... But I'm only one person. I can't protect them all. If I plant a tree here today, it's likely to dry up and die, or someone will come along and cut it down."

"No one will! I wouldn't let them."

"I was hoping you'd say that." She grinned like a sunbeam, only kinder. "Everywhere I plant trees, I find someone to look after them. Usually a kid like you, who still remembers how to hear what trees need. If you'll be a guardian for this tree and its sisters, if you'll gather up their seeds and plant them and grow new ones the way I just showed you, and if thousands of other guardians I find around the world do the same, then the forests will come back, and the world might have a chance."

"I'll do it," I said. Purpose tingled through me from head to toes, and I felt like I was glowing, just like the seeds. The old oak had been a good friend to me. I could be a good friend back.

All afternoon we planted sequoia seeds, in the park and along the road and in the broken pavement of abandoned lots. When I'd learned the trick of it, the Pinecone Lady said goodbye. She got back on her bike, and I raced to the middle of the empty road to watch her ride away—but by the time I got there, she was gone. She'd disappeared, as if she were never there at all.

But the seeds in my pocket stayed, and so did the trees we'd planted. By the next morning, the seedlings had grown two feet high. A week later, they were too high to see the top of. Soon, our trees shaded the park from the late summer sun. They took over abandoned farms. They grew up around the old strip mall, swallowing it up and delivering it back to the earth. They weren't fully grown yet, but even a young sequoia was a big, big tree. Everywhere I went, trees shot toward the sky.

That was the start. The rains didn't come back that year, or the year after, but eventually they did. Much later on, the scientists said it was the flourishing of trees, the restoration of the long-gone forests, that tipped us back into safety after we thought our planet was past the brink. And though folks like to pretend the Pinecone Lady is myth, I know better. For all these years, I've kept tending my trees just like she taught me. I keep on living that deepest, simplest truth: if we take good care of the forests, then they can take care of us.

ABOUT THE AUTHOR

Jo Miles writes optimistic science fiction and fantasy, and her stories have appeared in *Nature Futures*, *Analog*, *Diabolical Plots*, and more. You can find her online at www.jomiles.com and on Twitter as @josmiles. She lives in Maryland, where she is owned by two cats.

POWER TO THE PEOPLE

Kiera Lesley

SARAH stepped over the low front hedge and scuttled her way across the lawn until her shadow fell forward across the white gravel lining the side of Melissa's house. Further down, in the shadows cast by the fence, she could hear the scrunching of feet on the stones and the occasional metallic *thunk*. The contents of Sarah's hoodie pockets hung heavy and their hard points dug into her belly as she hurried to join in.

"You're late," Melissa snapped from where she stood at the rear corner of the house with the electrical panel already open. She held her phone light as a torch in one hand; the intermittent flashes of it lit her long, pale face and made her brown eyes look black. "This house isn't going to go rogue without you."

"Sorry, print took longer than I expected." Sarah said, fishing in her pockets for her offerings, all in white because that was the only colour filament she had.

"I told you not to do it right before." Melissa grabbed the parts from Sarah and inspected them in the light of her phone now propped inside the fuse box. "Mum said she'd be back from the gym at eight. That gives us half an hour to get this done and I don't want to get caught."

"I thought you said she'd be gone 'til nine?" Sarah shrugged when Melissa shot her a look. "Doesn't matter, the guides say you can do it in twenty minutes."

"Well, not if your friend doesn't print the bits you need until the second before she leav—shit." Melissa brandished one of the pieces: a cube half the width of a palm and riddled with channels and tiny loops. "This is the wrong one."

"What?"

"There was a version update on Monday. Why didn't you check you were working with the latest?"

Sarah stared at Melissa, stunned. Unbelievable. She was *helping* Melissa do this—something that was "between legal definitions" at best.

"Why didn't you make your own if it's so easy?"

Footsteps sounded on the far side of the plank fence behind them and they both fell silent, glaring at each other. They barely breathed until they heard the *click click* of a lighter and a green scent wafted over to them.

Melissa's shoulders sagged with relief.

"It's Mr Vanderknoop," Melissa muttered, leaning so close Sarah could smell her citrusy perfume. "Don't worry, I saw him linking his panels up the other weekend."

"At least you've got a close community transmission point," Sarah grumbled, still sore at Melissa. She hunched over and pulled up the chat app on her phone. She found the Solar Panel Rogues server and scrolled through the topic list: Set up rogue power at home. Designs. Manifesto—*If they won't get off fossils, we will!*

Tech support.

Sarah punched her question into the window as fast as her shaking thumbs could go.

Will last week's antenna design still work for connecting a late 90s unit?

The response came fast.

Definitely. Only difference is the new one is more slimline.

She flashed it to Melissa who scanned it once, grinned, and said, "Let's do this."

Melissa flicked off the mains switch—something so tiny, holding so much potential. Inside the house, everything fell black and quiet.

Sarah snapped the innocuous-looking plastic and metal pieces together and passed them to Melissa: rectenna, inverter, meter stealth override, neighbourhood overflow transmitter. The smell of solder filled the night air. Their fingers moved quickly, following directions memorised from weeks of reading, obsessing over design specs, and watching snippets of electronics videos online. Each stage containing just enough plausible deniability.

Headlights shone up the driveway. The pair froze again, their hands buried in their work and the house incriminatingly dark.

"She's not due back 'til eight!"

"It *is* eight." Melissa gestured to her phone's display with her chin.

"Shit!"

Sarah cut the pad of her thumb in her haste to reconnect everything, dimly aware that even though everyone said this process was super safe and anyone could do it there had been that one dickhead in Queensland who had probably died.

Too late now. Melissa pushed her thumb against the mains and flipped it on again.

"Please please please please."

Nothing.

The car's engine stopped, ticking as it cooled.

"Shit, we've stuffed it." Melissa turned on Sarah, crouched next to her against the brick wall as if that would hide them and what they had done. "You rushed it."

The headlights dimmed. The car door opened.

"*I*—? No, you're the one who hit the switch, this is your project. I didn't have to—"

The lights lit up all at once. A series of beeps echoed through the windows from various appliances resetting.

Sarah and Melissa shared a glance, joy and excitement, eyes shining in the shadows near the fuse box.

"We did it!" Melissa whispered in triumph.

Melissa's mum's footsteps tapped on the path.

The girls ran back in via the sliding glass door, feet loud on the gravel. The downlights inside shone bright—unaware that they were now running off 100-percent community-derived wireless-transferred solar as engineered by one genius in the Belgrave hills and released online, rather than the grid.

Melissa hurried to the microwave, the green numbers flashing zero, threw in a waiting bag of popcorn, and pressed the buttons. The bag started rotating, the microwave humming.

By the time Melissa's mum opened the front door, Sarah was settled on Melissa's grey U-shaped couch watching a TV blaring anime like it had never stopped. Melissa shook the bag, tore it open to release the steam, and offered some to Sarah.

"Thanks for helping," she said quietly. An olive branch.

Sarah paused. They'd been stressed and snappy, but they'd done it. Together.

She shrugged and took a handful of popcorn. "No worries."

"We'll do your place next week." Melissa turned back to the TV.

Sarah crunched, smiling. The fake butter tasted like victory.

ABOUT THE AUTHOR

Kiera Lesley lives in Melbourne, Australia with her partner and their retired racing greyhound. When not writing she enjoys tea, napping, heavy metal music, and hugs. You can find Kiera online at: www.chaptersinflux.com or on Twitter @KieraLesley.

THE KNELLS OF AGASSIZ

Holly Schofield

THE breeze is too gentle and too warm against Emma's cheeks as she steps out of the quad tiltrotor onto the gravel shoreline. The journey from more than seven hundred kilometres to the south has taken four hours. She sets the self-driving copter into standby mode with a swipe of her arm controls.

"Emma, what's wrong? Your GPS shows you've landed early. Over." Roger's worried voice crackles in her headset as the satellite signal travels all the way from Grise Fiord.

She toggles the switch with her tongue. "I decided to walk the last two kilometres."

Roger sputters. "It's dangerous to leave the copter's cabin, Em! What if the explosions—" The rest of his sentence is lost in a burst of static.

She tongues the off switch then mutters, "Tell me

something I don't know." This morning, she'd locked in the explosives programming herself before taking the copter.

Walking to the project site won't be easy. Spring thaw has come early, of course, and metre-wide creeks braid themselves across the stone-sprinkled delta that's splayed in front of her. But, there's no turning back.

Her sinuses are plugged again. She blows her nose over the creek, bush style, using two fingers of her mittened hand, and then begins this final journey, stepping over the narrowest of the creeks and feeling every one of her seventy years.

After a few minutes of walking, she begins to sweat. She spends a moment tying up her ponytail and lowering the heat in her parka. Today is "D-Day," as she's come to call it, the final phase of the project. The need to see Agassiz Ice Cap one more time, to witness what will be forever changed, has overridden the potential risks. Roger has always been too cautious.

However, she has perhaps overestimated her hiking abilities. She looks back at the copter, only a short distance behind her, where it waits patiently and silently until it's needed again. It could still easily take her to her destination but the desire to say goodbye to the ice cap, up close and in person, is too strong. She continues across the stony plain, one slow step at a time, with only the nasty chuckle of meltwater keeping her company.

While she hikes, she uses her heads-up display to check in on the project's progress. Roger has apparently given up trying to contact her. She accesses the daily calculations on the glacier's melt rate. Over the past decade, the Canadian government's underbudgeted recording methods have shown increasingly rapid ablation of all the Nunuvat glaciers and Agassiz is no exception. The Roger Ningiuk Foundation's more accurate measurements have shown that temperatures here on Ellesmere Island are actually averaging a horrifying 1.5 degrees higher than the federal agency has documented. She views other updates—all of today's figures are even worse than her modelling has predicted. She flicks the HUD off with an impatient hand.

After an hour's hard travel up the outwash and over the moss-covered boulders that form the moraine, she reaches the rotting snow at the glacier's edge. The SPF45 cream tastes of petroleum and civilization as she recoats her lips. She ignores her trembling leg muscles and turns to survey her footprints behind her. They're already filling with meltwater.

She scrambles up the incline over hardened snow that's been sculpted by the winter winds into the frozen waves of an insane ocean. Blurry tracks litter the snowy expanse beyond—a record of the many trips that she and Roger have made up here. Over the years, the arctic wind has lost its power to erase the signs of their presence.

Each step is a noisy shuffle over crystalline snow. She trudges onwards, remembering landmarks—here a stray boulder shaped like a wine barrel, there the place they camped for four days during a storm—the long stubborn history of surveying, measuring, and recording Agassiz's death knells.

Just as she considers then discards the idea of a short rest, her foot punches through the icy crust into softer snow below. A familiar jolt of pain shoots through her knee and she wobbles, off balance, until she can extricate her folding walking stick from her jacket's back pouch. She telescopes it out with a snap, braces herself, and pulls her leg back out. A quick stop, then, until the pulsating agony diminishes, her heart quiets, and a small degree of energy returns.

Once the quiet settles in, she hears a dull booming in the far distance, sounding like artillery in a distant war. The thought triggers a bitter smile. There is indeed a war, one she has fought for many years. And this trip is the final skirmish. She will not be returning.

Another boom, and then—in a minute—another, far above the dove-grey clouds overhead.

It won't be long until the explosions are only seconds apart.

Presumably by now Roger has discovered that she has changed the coding of the trial and he can no longer halt the progress. He'll also have figured out she's overridden the copter controls. She pictures his increasingly frantic radio calls to her and a familiar wash of guilt passes through her. Poor, faithful Roger. A decent person—too decent for her. He's better off without her and it will be so nice when she can rest, just rest.

She forces herself to walk again, but after a few more steps, she relents and reopens the connection. Roger's age-roughened voice is clear but faint. "OB1, do you read, come in? Em? Over, dammit." He'd given her the official title of Operations Manager, Biotech, calling himself Chief Engineer, despite there being only two of them on this project, not counting the hundred and twenty robots.

She tongues the switch. "Old Biddy One, over." Her voice is tinny and small in the immensity of the sky that surrounds her. The humour is weak but it's all she has to give him.

His voice is stern. "I can't stop the automated run now. You'll be right at ground zero soon. Please come back or else call the copter to come to you. Over."

"Not yet, Roger. This is something I have to do."

"Is it worth your life? Our life?" His voice is ragged. He's so upset he forgets the "over."

She plods along, berating herself for her slowness. The point of impact is still far ahead of her and, like all stages of this project, there's no time to waste. There has never been. Nunavut's glaciers are shrinking every second of every day. Roger could never see that, never understand what drove her to work on the project a hundred hours a week, to neglect her health and wellbeing.

"Goodbye, Roger." She severs the connection. The intensity of her voice causes a ptarmigan to burst forth from a nearby cluster of boulders. She's never seen one this far north nor one this skinny. It flies with ragged, dull feathers toward the glimmer of sun on the horizon. Inside one mitten, her fingers twitch but she stops before creating the wildlife diary entry.

There's no point. Not anymore. D-Day will change all that.

The clock in her HUD shows that she'd better hurry. One more kilometre to the centre of the project zone. Her sore knee pulls at each step as the imperfectly healed injury is called upon to support her weight. Twenty years ago, at the start of the project, when the warehouse in Grise Fiord was still shiny new and the launching ramp only a sketch on her computer, a prototype glider had exploded prematurely, sending a small but deadly shard of wood into her knee cap.

She had fallen to the factory floor, her cry as much from exaltation as from pain: the force of impact of the wood scrap anecdotally serving to prove the success of the experiment. The blue-streaked sawdust, a by-product salvaged from a robot-run mill in a Northwest Territories forest wiped out by mountain pine beetles, would be a significant cost savings. Roger's stress-induced breakdown later that day had not prevented Emma from soldiering on with their research and neither had his lengthy recovery in the hospital. And, indeed, the coarse sawdust and seawater mixture had later shown to be structurally sound enough to form a mixture as hard as concrete, yet soft enough to pulverize during explosion.

She pauses, remembering one more thing. In the years that followed, whenever she combated Ellesmere's short hot summers by wearing khaki shorts to the factory, Roger would draw circles around the scar tissue on her knee with his thick fingers. She'd brush his hand away, berating him to get back to work. With a start, she realizes he doesn't do that anymore.

More rumbling followed by a boom as another glider explodes high above the leaden clouds. Only half a kilometre now. Exhaustion tugs at her. There are several ways this day can turn out—a misfiring glider can obliterate her instantly, her own frailty can send her sliding into a gully to drown in meltwater, a dozen other tragedies. They're all immaterial—the cardiologist has given her less than a month to live. But, at least, the trials can continue—Roger will see to that, even after she's gone.

In the past two decades, she'd spent substantial amounts of Roger's money in attempts to save the glaciers. Early projects included mimicking the Peruvian man who had painfully spread sawdust on an Andes glacier, wheelbarrow after wheelbarrow full. She'd even tried painting the terminus of the glacier in white paint to offer a more reflective surface. Two trips to Sweden on Roger's money to study a snow machine operation that was spraying a glacier above an Olso ski hill had eventually determined that it, also, was too small-scale for her needs.

Finally, water and wood had shown the way. Two of nature's most common materials, frozen together to make a surprisingly resilient material.

The hardest part of mixing the seawater and sawdust then molding it aerodynamically had been convincing people that it wouldn't be a repeat of the famous WWII failed experiments. The substance, known as pykrete in the 1940s, was to be used as an aircraft carrier in the Arctic but had repeatedly melted at inopportune times. Emma's concoction was chemically different, as was the application—gliders shaped like thick paper airplanes.

The only easy part had been obtaining the seawater. No one objects to the foundation sucking it up from the ocean, not after the Grise Fiord shoreline rose a dozen feet within recent memory. And the salt in the seawater is an added advantage, helping snow crystals form almost as well as silver iodide but without its degree of environmental damage.

She stops to examine a dark spot on the snow. Scat, at first glance—her tired heart thumps, although she has not seen a wolf or polar bear in two years. But, no, it's just a stone covered with *Polytrichum strictum*, the moss that's spreading northward in the new Arctic warmth, its spruce-green colour working to decrease the albedo and therefore accelerate the glaciers' melt rate. If she squints, she can pick out particulates in the nearby snow, too, sprinkled like black pepper.

Another rumble, this time almost straight overhead. She pictures the robots in the factory molding the gliders, the gliders speeding off the factory's launch ramps, all in a continuous progression, over and over. The gliders are empty of payload, of course: the seawater-wood pulp mixture they're made from *is* the payload. A GPS-triggered explosion and then icy wood pulp falling, falling into the cloud layer overhead, forming seeds—seeds of either destruction or cautious hope.

Her HUD beeps as the preset GPS coordinates are

reached.

Ground zero.

She stops immediately, leaning on her stick, knee throbbing. Her neck pops as she angles her head back. High above, each cloud is gathering moisture, growing heavy, pregnant with snow. An idealistic concept, almost a concept of a concept, that such a procedure would result in an insulating blanket of snow protecting the dying glacier under her feet.

It's amazing they've brought the project along this far. Even if it fails now, even if a glider were to strike her in the next few moments, Roger deserves a minute-by-minute report. He has never stopped asking her to marry him and she has never said yes. This project was too important to jeopardize with a relationship, too time-consuming to allow her to have a life. How can she rest, how can anyone rest, until the glaciers are saved? She activates the radio. "I'm here, Rog. Nothing yet."

His reply is instantaneous. "How are you, Em? Really."

"Good." Her nose is a constant drip, her knee is on fire, and she's so tired, she could lie down on the snow crust and sleep instantly. "How's it look at your end?"

Roger speaks in a rush. "All prelims are favourable. Too soon to tell, though."

"Your grandpa would be proud, Rog." And he would have been.

"Doesn't make things right." His voice is quiet. Roger's Inuit grandfather had spent his final years chastising Roger for the success of his luxury ecotourism company and the resulting degradation of Ellesmere Island's many habitats. Roger's investment in Emma's project has done little to assuage his guilt but Emma has been desperate enough for funding over the years to continue to let him try. Her own guilt pulses hotly within her. She rubs her scarred knee through her thick snowpants. She'll need to sit down soon, then lie down. The thought of resting consumes her.

More booms overhead. And then—she squints to make sure—a sheet of snow is ghosting toward her over the barren plain. It reaches her quickly and small, hard pellets of ice sting her cheeks. They're a far cry from the moist fluffy flakes that fall in southern Canada, but it's *snow:* beautiful, wonderful, *insulating* snow plinking against her hood like miniature silver bells.

"It works," she whispers. "It goddamn works." The grains of ice grow into tiny drifts at her feet. Small dots of sawdust settle like damp yellow powder. It's as if land and ocean are reuniting with the ancient ice below.

Eventually, she can no longer feel her toes and she leans heavily on the stick. It sinks into the soft icepack, almost toppling her.

"I've hacked the copter. It's on its way," Roger says. Almost instantly, she can hear distant blades wicking the air.

Her heart rate is so rapid she can hardly distinguish beats. Suddenly, she knows what she wants to do.

Quickly, she removes her hood and puts her headset by her boots. She loosens her ponytail and shakes her head, spreading her hair over her collar.

With an impish smile, she tilts back her head.

And sticks out her tongue.

First one flake, and then two, three, ten, they land and melt. The taste is sour wood pulp and tangy seaweed and missed chances and unrealized dreams. The soft *whupwhupwhup* of the copter grows louder. Roger's voice squawks plaintively from the discarded headset.

The flakes grow thicker. It's indisputable: the project is a success and can now be replicated on other glaciers. She'll need to get that heart surgery. And a knee replacement. The next decades will be busy ones.

Snow begins to twist around her in wild fury. Her doubt and guilt and exhaustion swirl away with it.

She bends and picks up the headset so that she's ready when the copter arrives. There's no time to waste.

ABOUT THE AUTHOR

Holly Schofield travels through time at the rate of one second per second, oscillating between the alternate realities of city and country life. Her short stories have appeared in *Analog*, *Lightspeed*, *Escape Pod*, and many other publications throughout the world. She hopes to save the world through science fiction and homegrown heritage tomatoes. Find her at hollyschofield.wordpress.com.

GOOD HUNTING

M. Darusha Wehm

KARIN Eklund sauntered casually toward the staff entrance to the Gyrodigital building. The sun had been down for nearly an hour, but Gyrodigital was one of those companies that expected long hours from their employees. No one would think twice about someone arriving at this time.

If anyone had stopped to ask her for ID, she'd have been caught immediately. Each Gyrodigital employee had an unbranded swipe card and a separate ID with their name, photo, and department listed under a huge Gyrodigital logo, which a security officer could match to the data on the employee's record. But she didn't have one of those. She only had a generic RFID card that had been loaded with fake electronic credentials, and the reader happily beeped when she swiped it over the sensor. There were no human security staff nearby to double-check, so she slipped into the building undetected.

She tapped a beat out on the electronic tattoo on her arm to open an audio channel to her spotter, then subvocalized, "Step one, complete."

• • •

Officer Taylor Demir watched as the intruder entered Gyrodigital's offices. A combination of private and law enforcement drone-camera footage played over Demir's vision, the heads-up display projected on the windscreen of the patrol car. Demir's implants connected them to the automated car's system so intimately that, had an emergency situation arisen, they could have taken manual control of the vehicle in an instant. But they didn't expect to have to make any deviation from the mission—the Gyrodigital bust was the department's top priority today.

Their visuals switched over to interior cameras as the tiny drones followed the intruder as she coolly walked toward Gyrodigital's server room. Demir gave the woman her due— she looked for all the world to be an office jockey stuck working late. There was nothing suspicious about her whatsoever. Demir knew better, though, and ordered the car to increase speed.

• • •

Karin swiped into the server room and shivered as the sheen of sweat on her face cooled in the room's heavy air conditioning. The air smelled wrong, and she guessed that Gyrodigital was using the cheap, effective but environmentally destructive coolant that had been banned years ago. It would be a minor infraction compared to the rest of the corporation's crimes against the environment. Which was why she was here.

It wasn't enough to tell the world that one of the largest producers of electronic goods was cheating on their carbon returns. Someone had to stop them, and that was why she was sitting in front of a terminal at nine at night, typing furiously into the admin portal to try to gain access to Gyrodigital's deployment system.

• • •

The patrol car's ETA system showed nearly ten minutes until they would arrive at Gyrodigital, so Demir pulled up some files. Facial recognition had gotten a hit on the intruder: Karin Eklund.

Several arrests at protests in support of the UN Resolution on Global Carbon Emission Regulations some years previously, but no convictions. However, there was evidence that Eklund was linked to a radical action group that had stolen several large corporations' internal documents showing that their official Climate Impact Statements had been falsified.

Demir flipped though the dossier, text and images overlaid on their vision as they sped through the city streets toward Gyrodigital's head office. The data on Eklund had dried up nearly two years ago. It was as if she'd dropped off the face of the earth, but here she was, caught on one of Demir's microdrone cameras that had followed her into the Gyrodigital server room.

Demir watched in real time as Eklund hacked her way into the system.

Your destination is on the left, the car's audio system informed them, and Demir cleared their vision.

Showtime.

• • •

Karin's heart thudded as she typed, time feeling much slower than its one-second-per-second rate. After a relative eternity, she saw the string of text she'd been waiting for: ACCESS GRANTED. She entered the commands that would shut down Gyrodigital's off-books manufacturing plants around the world; the ones still pumping out toxic waste, the ones still burning coal for power, the ones still pouring bywaste into the world's lakes and rivers and oceans.

"Cops are here," the voice in her earpiece said calmly, and she subvocalized an acknowledgment but kept typing. She only had a small window of time before legal processes would shut down all online access from this building, so she forced herself to focus on the task at hand.

• • •

Demir entered Gyrodigital through the front door, their uniform and badge scanned by the building's automated security. All doors automatically unlocked for them, and they strode down the main hall. Before passing the server room, they pushed open the door.

"Nice to meet you, Eklund," they said to the woman furiously typing at the terminal. "You probably have about five minutes before the court order will freeze Gyrodigital's servers."

"Got it," Karin said without turning away from the screen. "Good hunting."

Demir said, "Thanks," and continued down the hallway to the offices where a board meeting was in progress. They brought up the electronic warrant on their handheld projector as they opened the door to the boardroom. It would be the first significant bust of the new climate protection laws: the CEO and board of Gyrodigital, all in clear violation of the globally enforceable regulations. Some of them might even end up in prison, and surely the company would be broken up, with increased oversight on all its production facilities.

"Good evening," Demir said to the roomful of stunned executives. "You're under arrest."

ABOUT THE AUTHOR

M. Darusha Wehm is the Nebula Award-nominated and Sir Julius Vogel Award winning author of the interactive fiction game *The Martian Job*, as well as twelve novels, several poems, and many short stories. Originally from Canada, Darusha lives in Wellington, New Zealand after spending several years sailing the Pacific.

SOLITUDE, IN SILENT SUN

Mike Adamson

CHÉRIE Duvalon was second-generation Terran, and proud of it.

She sat on hard-packed sand and squinted against its white glare. The afternoon sun dried her stretch thermal sheath and crystallized salt on her skin. Her fair hair fluttered in the breeze, and her diving helmet, weight belt, and fins lay on the sharp sand at her side. She loved the long, corrugated coast from once-drowned Montpellier to Nîmes, while knowing it used to be a steep contour change far inland. The rise of the oceans as the twenty-first century wore on had swamped the low-lying Camargue region between the eastern and western branches of the Rhone, and much more. Over 7000 square kilometres had been lost to the sea locally, and the area now constituted a warm, shallow bank where the life reintroduced since the 2170s was thriving.

Chérie's family thought she was coming out here to meet a boy, and she was happy with the misconception—the truth, that she simply needed time away from them, was the bitterer. They told her the coast was not safe, that outlaw gangs haunted the marshes, wind-tossed dunes, and salt creeks, plying their illegal trade in black market tech, and she took them seriously ... But the natural beauty was the balm she needed.

She loved her family, but ... Young people were often accused of not seeing the bigger picture, yet sometimes they saw with a scope, a clarity, unfettered by the necessities of day-to-day life. This put their worldview at odds with that of their parents, and Chérie was disturbed by just such *details*.

She sighed, and let the calm view soothe her. The aquamarine sea faded onto the shore in gentle waves, under a sky of the most intense blue imaginable; the first dune rose a hundred metres at her back, and she was immersed in near silence. Birds soared, hovering on the warm wind, their cries sweet, and it seemed impossible to imagine every higher life form in this place had been lovingly returned since not long before the birth of her parents.

Her grandparents had been born around 2160 at space city Europa, one of the cluster of complexes out at L5, trailing the moon in its orbit, during the near century when the planet was inimical to human life. Soaring temperatures, skewed O_2/CO_2 balances, and mass extinction of all higher organisms set in just after 2100—since then, the environment had favoured only extremophiles. But a day came when the great terraforming initiative gained traction, the sun shield out in space modulated incoming radiance, and the global program of reseeding brought life back—millions of species remained to be introduced, but Earth was once more habitable. The remnants of humankind streamed back from the black, to cautiously reawaken long-dead cities and return the sleeping world to its former stature, though this time with technologies geared to the natural processes of the planet—not against it.

Chérie was a troubled child of the twenty-third century. Knowing she belonged to a species capable of exterminating the very life systems she loved was hard enough, but knowing old ways threatened to return was worse. Small-steaders, like her family, were at times hard-pressed to get by with the kind of tech that did not damage the environment, and here and there it was more convenient to burn that rubbish, fail to recycle, or fall back on illegal chemistry to improve yield or ward off pests—also reintroduced as vital components of the wider ecosystem.

Her father had spoken in these terms and gestured to the new idyllic shores and shallows as evidence that it didn't matter if *one* person did not live up to the covenant all humans now had with their world. Despite her youth, Chérie knew there was no such thing as *only one* person failing to follow through—if anyone slacked off, *everyone* would, and they were not yet three generations into the rehabilitation of the planet.

And he had more than spoken of it. She had seen trash disappear, not stored and recycled properly but simply *disappear*, and it did not take a genius to know he had taken it out into deep water beyond the old shoreline and dumped it. She had seen receipts from suppliers of maricultural chemistry, suppliers she did not recognize and could not find in reputable databases. What was it he burned in a steel drum on a surface float above their habitat steading?

She had tried to talk to her mother about her misgivings, but been brushed off with platitudes about things "looking up" for them. They were producing excellent yields, supplying alginates and protein biomass to the big combines that synthesized food for the rejuvenating cities; the money was good and the new green economy was thriving. It seemed her mother was tacitly saying they just needed to get through the next few years, and then they would be able to follow the letter of the regulations, instead of merely their spirit. They just needed to get that bit farther ahead …

What was Chérie meant to think, or feel? This schism, between all she had learned of the painstaking, century-long rehabilitation of the planet, and her father's behaviour when it came to living up to the responsibilities each person had to their world, was enough to drive her to distraction. It *hurt* to know he was releasing carbon into the sky, using chemistry that may harm life, merely to get ahead of their neighbours. It was a hurt she was finding harder and harder to bear. But to act would make her ungrateful.

She brooded in the afternoon, only the trickle of waters and the cries of birds, the shush of blowing sand, to disturb her. Should she go to the authorities? Tackle him directly? She was afraid to ... He had never been violent, but Maurice Duvalon could be a stern man, and quite set in his ways. He was a scientific farmer of the sea who prided himself on being an old-fashioned Gallic businessman, hard-nosed and willing to make less-than-popular choices in order to build for their personal future. If she reported him, she risked sabotaging her family fortunes. At the very least she would be disloyal to her parents. Yet, if she did not, she facilitated the sabotage of the fragile new life systems of Earth.

Barely three generations back on the planet, and *some people* were already breaking it again.

Had she not heard her mother speak in hushed tones of the authorities sending people back into space, throwing them off the planet, if they were found wanting? Would the old cities out there become prisons? Then why would her father be so stupid? She could not really credit the notion, but ... *maybe* it was true. Or was it just a tale to make children behave? She sighed, remembered hours spent in her room, tapping at her tablet, seeking some support or refutation of such disturbing thoughts. She had found nothing, which left her in turmoil.

Being out here in the air and sun was her distraction from such uncomfortable reality, but today she clung to the peace just a little longer than was wise.

The first she knew of trouble was the scrabble of tires up

in the dunes, a flicker of movement in the corner of her eye. Figures moved among the rim of thorny grasses and salt bush, and she caught her breath: abduction was a lucrative sideline for criminals.

Heart in mouth, she was up in moments. A hundred metres was not much head start, but she scooped up the plastic helmet, dropped it over her head, and closed it with a hard contact of machined latches. The neck seal inflated and she grabbed her belt and fins to run, her adrenaline surging.

A dozen figures pounded down the dune onto the level sand. Chérie splashed into the sea, went hip deep, and twisted. She plunged in backward, threw the belt around her loins, and shoved feet into fins. As her pursuers hit the water's edge she flipped over, went under, and dolphin-kicked hard into the flickering aqua.

The bioorganic rebreather built into the helmet delivered her oxygen the moment she was under, and the clear forward half of the helmet gave her unrestricted visibility. She bobbed to the surface a minute later to find the smugglers milling shoulder deep, not equipped to follow. She sighed, heart steadying, and duck-dived to follow the bed she knew so well to a gully, soar gently into it, and make her way south away from the land across what had once been green country.

If people's sense of responsibility had faded already, what could they expect from tomorrow? The smugglers proved the point: renegades, making fast profits the old way, and it was not good enough. Chérie's young face was set with resolve as she crossed the new corals and seagrass meadows, following the slope into cooler, blue waters, and when she found, ahead, the habitat lights of the family mariculture steading, one of dozens of small farming operations threaded along the coast to work the rich new Camargue Bank, her mind was made up.

It was made up even more as she saw a small robotic submersible working the kelp beds where they grew alginates, and knew beyond any doubt it was treating the great fronds with substances ultimately harmful to the organisms with which they shared this place. She scowled behind her faceplate, alighted on her knees to watch the machine moving among the kelp, and shook her head. The fish and mollusks that used these beds as a new and vigorous habitat would themselves sicken and die, perhaps first passing on broken genes, which called for yet more intervention to repair ...

She steeled her resolve, her stomach turning at the prospect, but she knew she had no choice. And if she heard anything less than she needed to, it would be the gendarmes. Loyalty be damned, if the last hundred and sixty years had taught the human race anything, it was that some priorities were not negotiable. She *would* tackle her father.

Life came first.

ABOUT THE AUTHOR

Mike Adamson holds a doctoral degree from Flinders University of South Australia. After early aspirations in art and writing, Mike returned to study and secured degrees in both marine biology and archaeology. Mike has been a university educator since 2006, has worked in the replication of convincing ancient fossils, is a passionate photographer, a master-level hobbyist, and a journalist for international magazines. Short fiction sales include to *Hybrid Fiction, Weird Tales, Abyss and Apex, Daily Science Fiction, Compelling Science Fiction,* and *Nature Futures.* Mike has placed some 115 stories to date.

GHOST FISHING

William Delman

I'D just finished inspecting the bilge, rudder control, and the levels on our batteries when Captain Ellen Stubb's voice rang out over the intercom. "Pam, I need you up here."

In the *Incentive*'s wheelhouse, Stubb was bent forward in her blue and white flannel, ominous as Hokusai's Great Wave. She was glaring at the *Earth Crisis*, a big, modified dive support vehicle maybe two kilometres off our stern bow. With remote subs, a saturation diving system, and a heavy crane, *Crisis* was newer and more robust than any other boat in the Bering Sea. She represented the future according to her corporate backers, capable of harvesting more abandoned fishing gear and plastic trash in a year than most boats could in three.

Unfortunately, this bright exemplar of sustainable capitalism was on our salvage grounds. Again. Everyone in the fleet knew *Crisis* had a bad habit of ignoring claim boundaries, and she seemed to violate ours more than most.

"These people don't quit," I said.

Stubb's hand crashed down on the dash, scattering dust motes to the air.

"Claim jumpers don't quit unless you make them quit." Stubb pointed at the battery gauges. "Thought you fixed these."

"Must be another short. I'll track it down."

"Fuel cells got enough juice for a hard run?"

I nodded. "As long as we're running home."

Stubb grabbed the sideband mic and thumbed down the talk switch. "Piper, get topside. Then come see me."

The *Incentive*'s diver sounded annoyed and confused over the radio. "Captain? I'm working a big knot of ghost gear down here. I got nets, lines, even a crab pot. You want me to quit?"

Stubb's eyes glinted hard as January ice. "Ghosts ain't going anywhere."

She slammed the mic back into its bracket and glanced at me. "Go give Santiago a hand on the deck. After everything's secure, I want everyone up here for a meeting."

She was still glaring at the *Crisis* when I left.

Over two hundred years of "ghost" gear—lost fishing nets, ropes, and other recyclable polymers—littered the Bering Sea floor. At current, post-peak-oil market prices, what had once been garbage now brought in millions. Failed towns, throttled by fishing moratoriums, were being reborn as crews raced to pull "ghosts" from the sea. I'd come north after getting my MS, bursting with righteous energy, only to find that, for most, this business wasn't about saving the planet; it was about keeping families fed and boats running.

Two years as *Incentive*'s engineer had tempered my ecological idealism. Still, *Crisis* impressed me. She was getting the job done.

Out on the deck, Santiago was checking our manila lines for rot. "Make ready for ramming speed?" He grinned, grey beard shimmering with spray around chapped lips.

"Captain ordered Piper to quit fishing. I've never seen her this mad."

As if on cue, an orange lift bag surfaced with a yellow flag attached. Piper would be up in ten minutes. Four more bags followed the first one, all stuffed with recovered nylon netting, or rope, or other treasure.

Santiago clapped his hands. "Let's salvage what we can."

We dragged the bags from the sea until Piper surfaced. He started talking the second he got his mask off. "Rat's nest under us must weigh a ton. We're talking serious money."

Santiago pointed at the *Crisis*. "Captain's got other concerns."

We crowded into the wheelhouse. Piper scowled and rubbed the lines his mask had left on his face. Santiago was quiet.

"Captain, we're sitting on a jackpot," Piper said, his tone sharp.

Stubb remained unmoved. "Jumpers need to learn, Piper.

They can't keep taking what's ours. Tape together a couple diving charges. You're going hunting."

Then she looked at Santiago. "You and Pam are going to move the dive boat to the deck, paint it black, and pull the radar target enhancer."

"That'll make it almost impossible to spot," I said.

Stubb nodded. "Yup."

Piper stomped off toward his quarters while we scudded back to the deck.

"What did the captain mean, 'go hunting?' What's she planning?" I asked.

"You know Piper was a frogman?" Santiago said. "Diving charges can do some serious damage to a hull. Maybe worse, depending on where you put them."

"No way," I said. "She wouldn't."

Santiago finished lowering the dive boat with the crane, shrugged. "Captain says, 'paint.' We paint."

"Sure, but we still have a choice, right?" I said.

"Choice? Sure." He pointed to the paintbrush in my hand.

That night, alone in the galley, I cleaned and thought. When Stubb first hired me, she showed me the old-fashioned cork board she kept over her coffee maker. There were a dozen photos tacked up, mostly portraits with names written in black Sharpie.

"Each one of these people, here or not, lasted at least a season. That makes them more than crew. We take care of each other, everyone gets paid, and maybe the ocean gets a little cleaner. Understand?"

Remembering that conversation, I frowned. Stubb thought we needed to send a message, protect what was ours. Maybe she was right, even if it didn't feel right.

The clock read one when Santiago woke me in my bunk. "Need you on deck."

Piper came out suited up for a dive with a black canvas duffle slung over one shoulder.

"Sure about this?" Santiago said.

Piper nodded once, hard.

They looked at me. I opened my mouth, closed it again, and watched my silence deform into a decision.

With *Incentive* running under navigation lights and nothing else, the matte black dive boat vanished like a shadow into the darkness. Santiago and I stood by the port side gunwale looking at the *Crisis*, only a kilometre away. For the first time since I'd stepped on board, I felt nauseated.

"Guess that's it." Santiago pulled his halogen flashlight from his pocket. He held it over the side, and started clicking. It took me a few seconds to recognize the two-letter codes: NF, PP.

You are running into danger. Keep clear.

In the near pitch, there was zero chance the *Crisis*, or Stubb, would miss the signal.

"What are you doing?" I was incredulous.

Santiago shrugged. "The right thing, maybe. You keep quiet, walk away, maybe Stubb will let you stay on after."

My nausea vanished. I had a choice, and I made it, adding

my light to his.

ABOUT THE AUTHOR

William's work has appeared in *Little Blue Marble*, *Daily Science Fiction*, *Kraxon*, *The Arcanist*, *New Orbit*, *The Selene Quarterly*, *Write Ahead/The Future Looms*, and many other fine publications. He longs for the days when Pandemic was only a board game, and hopes that you and yours are well.

DIGITAL PYRE

A. P. Howell

EILEEN stared at the dialog box. Such a little thing standing between her and an irrevocable act of destruction. Did she want to delete records, massive quantities of records painstakingly maintained by herself and the archivists who had preceded her? "OK" and "Cancel" didn't seem like adequate choices. This was an essay question, not true or false.

For months, Eileen had combed through the digital records in her care. Images of rare books and manuscripts; scans of twentieth-century documents too delicate for routine handling; a six-linear-foot collection, digitized in its entirety courtesy of a monetary donation tied to the materials; the born-digital records of scientists, the historical significance of which might not be clear for decades.

So much material held in just one institution, and so little of it to be saved. So much material, so many servers, so much energy used on- and off-site.

S.O.S., they called it: "selection on steroids" and a professional cri de coeur. Eileen had made her decisions and then sabotaged routine backups, carefully excluding most of the archived materials in her care. She suppressed error warnings and held her breath waiting for an email from IT that never came.

Archivists' power was distributed. That was usually a disadvantage, a barrier to institutional clout and collective bargaining, with precarious employment complicating community ties. But that left archivists widespread, working in many different public and private institutions. It also meant the cultivation of professional networks divorced from geography. That could translate to slacktivism—but sometimes it evolved into Slacktivism.

They'd all had training in distributed action, informal but high stakes. Crowdfunding to cover strangers' medical expenses; donations to make professional conferences slightly more affordable for the most marginalized; outreach to communities ignored by or mistrustful of collecting institutions; hashtags to amplify and focus debate; desperate ad hoc, cross-disciplinary projects to save public climate data at risk of destruction by a hostile government.

Word of mouth, whisper networks, conference hallway tracks, shared documents with many editors: this was simply the way things worked. The way they shared knowledge, sorted individuals or institutions into categories of helpful or harmful, the way things got done.

Eileen had met some of her coconspirators in person, through national and regional conferences, workshops, and the enduring ties binding former classmates and colleagues. But others remained avatars and author headshots, friends of friends bound together in a web of trust and professional unity.

She tried not to think of parallels to terrorist cells, though she suspected they'd soon hear that analysis. How else would media contextualize a massive loss of data? The coordinated deletions were clearly a plan—even without the accompanying manifesto, it would be obvious the event was no accident—and that made those responsible coconspirators. They were doing the right thing, but she still couldn't reconcile *coconspirator* with her self-image.

Instead, Eileen thought of a years-old visualization, a network diagram identifying Paul Revere based upon social connections. Setting aside all the deeply problematic aspects of the American project and the mythology surrounding national identity, it comforted her to consider herself part of a revolutionary tradition rather than one of isolated groups dedicated to violence. Eileen contemplated the essays, posts, and comments to this effect primed to go live. She'd already seen a few of them floating around the web in advance, heartfelt and strategic.

Eileen had printed out a lot of personal documents. Paper was easy to take care of and (often) long-lasting, whereas bits were notoriously difficult to preserve, migrate, and access. Intellectually, she knew a picture of Sophie, age five, was safer in the frame on her desk than floating around the cloud as a JPG. Having the picture on her desk at work and at home made it unlikely that she would lose both, barring a regional natural disaster.

The sort of regional natural disaster that was becoming increasingly common, as hurricanes became more severe, sea levels rose, and continents burned. Sensible disaster protocols called for geographically dispersed electronic backups. But did it matter that one had technically done one's fiduciary duty, if the collection fell victim to a flood in New Jersey and a wildfire in California?

Nowhere was safe, and it would only get worse. They'd already passed several points of no return, with so many aspects of twenty-first-century life unsustainable. The average individual couldn't exert a meaningful impact on the climate. A focus on personal empowerment was one of the cleverest, most insidious lies of the Anthropocene.

The average individual couldn't do much. Neither could a loosely connected group of archivists. But they did what they could. That was, maybe, the most important aspect of this action: a tiny step taken in the right direction, a tiny cooling of some data centres. Maybe, a tiny way to hurt the powerful. Maybe, a tiny way to remind people what they were going to lose, to spur them to consider those losses, material and emotional. To spur them to prepare themselves for the future that could no longer be prevented.

Eileen deleted the contents of her social media accounts.

Years' worth of posts, comments, photos, and videos. Mementoes and memory triggers, all gone from the web. All unavailable for amateur data mining. A copy existed, along with the electronic histories of everyone else involved in the action. Hard drives sat on a lawyer's desk, who did not know the contents or the reason she was shortly going to earn her retainer. But no one who had deleted material planned to ever recover it for personal use. They were walking the walk.

A lot of social media was going to disappear—some of it permanently—and that might garner quick, widespread attention. But other companies would lose a lot of data, and there might be panicked knock-on effects. The economy would take a hit. Eileen felt sorry about that; the consequences would fall most heavily on those who could least afford it. But still, this was the right thing to do.

Being an archivist didn't mean saving everything; it never had. The job was all about making choices. What to collect, who to collect it from, and how well to describe, preserve, and make it accessible. How long to retain it. Archivists always made those decisions within constraints: physical space and institutional mission and funding and headcount and a thousand other factors.

Eileen and her coconspirators had just decided to (finally, belatedly) prioritize the climate impact of their digital data. It was not so different from deaccessioning materials outside of a collection's scope ... except it felt entirely different. They wielded professional ethics unilaterally, not within defined institutional constraints.

She pasted in the new social media updates: agreed-upon verbiage, hashtags, and contact information for the press. For once, maybe news stories about archives would quote actual archivists. The posts included links to multiply-mirrored sites hosting the manifesto and detailed breakdowns of the data destroyed and the anticipated impact, economic and climatic.

> *The planet is burning. In some places, it is literally on fire. With this action, we burn a piece of our past to save our future.*

Eileen regretted never again being able to zoom in on that photo of Sophie, never again to add filters or colour correct the red-eye. But she had always regretted the precarity of her daughter's future.

Some griefs were more compelling than others, and demanded action as well as mourning.

ABOUT THE AUTHOR

A. P. Howell has worked as an archivist, ice cream scooper, webmaster, and data wrangler. She lives with her spouse, their two kids, and a dog who hates groundhogs, close enough to Philadelphia to complain about SEPTA while enjoying an abundance of good cheesesteaks. Her short fiction has appeared in *Daily Science Fiction*, *Eighteen: Stories of Mischief and Mayhem*, and *Community of Magic Pens*, and she can be found online at aphowell.com.

CHOOSE YOUR BATTLEGROUND

Andrew Leon Hudson

THE first time I tried to regreen our town, I was sixteen. I got sentenced to 150 hours of community service, which Trev told the judge was ironic, seeing as we'd been trying to do the community a service in the first place, and it had only taken us a fraction of that.

Trev got 300 hours.

According to the prosecutor, we were guilty of vandalism, disturbing the peace, and unlicensed dumping on city property—there's nothing like a bit of creative sentencing. Seeing as what we *specifically* did was reappropriate the cast-offs when our local sports centre returfed their playing field and covered 7000 square metres of Main Street with reasonable quality grass, Trev wondered why they didn't try to pin drug dealing on us too.

I kept my head down, did my time, and got back to my studies. Trev spent his downtime planning how to do our guerrilla activism better in future.

• • •

The second time I tried to regreen our town, I was getting ready to leave for college.

Every autumn, our town has a harvest festival—what town doesn't? There's a big parade, all the local schools and businesses decorate floats and drive slowly through the crowds, then everyone follows them out to Manor Park on the outskirts of town, where the mayor and his wife give speeches and the corporate sponsors lay on a giant buffet. That year, as soon as everyone was out of the way, we showed up in a truck Trev had "borrowed" from a nearby farm and dumped a layer of earth all the way from Bakerstown Lane to Humbolt Street, right past the new shopping mall, peppered with the fastest-growing variety of bamboo seeds you could bulk order online.

By the time the first people started drifting back home in the early evening, a mini forest almost a foot high blocked access to the supermarket. By the time the council got its act together and arranged a harvest, the bamboo stood over shoulder high.

When Trev hits on an idea he likes, he doesn't let it go easily.

It was great, but it still got torn up, and no one had any doubt about who was responsible. About a week later the police traced the seed purchase to Trev. His parents got a knock on the door, and this time Trev got six months inside.

He kept my name out of it, bless him.

And by the time he got out, I'd changed my degree to Ecology and Agriculture.

• • •

The third time I tried to regreen our town, I decided to do it on the up-and-up.

My graduation project was on urban farming, but it wasn't a hypothetical thing, it was as grounded as they come. I based the whole thing on the old multilevel car park in back of the shopping mall. I'd gotten hold of the original blueprints and designed a self-sustaining vertical farm based on it: on the roof I'd put rain collectors to ease the water burden, and solar panels to help power the grow lights; it'd have eight floors of fruit and veg production, some of it hydroponic, some semitraditional.

I had a whole business model prepared. I'd start a company, rent four floors to small local farmers, four we'd run ourselves, and we'd sell all goods strictly within the immediate vicinity for a minimal carbon footprint. I'd divide the one floor left over into private plots for members of the public—there hadn't been a proper allotment in town since before I was born, and as part of my project I'd canvassed residents and farmers, pitched the idea, and got letters of support and interest from all sides. I even secured a loan agreement from my bank, conditional on the council agreeing to sell me the site.

Instead, at the mayor's encouragement, the council signed the site over to a property developer, to knock it down and build a bunch of trendy new apartments.

Happily, Trev was on parole at the time, so he got me drunk, showed me all his latest tattoos, and told me I was a fool for abandoning the tried and tested strategy of blocking streets with earth and plant matter. Given that his latest spell inside was for doing exactly that, yet again, you'd think I'd have had the sense to ignore him.

• • •

The fourth time I tried to regreen our town, I decided to meet Trev halfway.

We cruised around town, scouting the ideal location. *Not* in front of the town hall, or the mall, none of the places Trev thought would make the biggest statement—for all his teenaged insights, he'd never quite clicked that he kept choosing the wrong targets.

No, I was looking for something else.

Somewhere out on the edge of town would be good. Not the best neighbourhood, the kind of place where the road surface is three-quarters pothole, and the paving slabs look like someone took a sledgehammer to them. Not many jobs, not many cars, because no one can afford to fix or run them anymore.

We found just the place.

One night, we rolled up in another borrowed truck, tilted the back, and carefully filled the whole street with earth from sidewalk to sidewalk—Trev's *modus operandi* to a tee. But this time, we planted vegetable gardens in front of every house, and leaflets in the mailboxes with a plan of the plots and some basic guidelines, so the new lucky owners would know what to do with them. I also included a calculation of how much money they'd save if they kept them going—you'd be surprised.

The finishing touch? Two strips of turf unrolled over those mangy sidewalks for the kids to play on. Complete with a sign reading "Please Walk on The Grass."

The town council went nuts, of course. But would you believe that, when they finally sent workmen in to clear up "the mess," the residents locked arms and refused to let them through? The mayor himself went to placate them and explain how it was a misuse of civic property, but he wasn't very pleased to see the local TV station show up to record the event, and didn't have good answers for why a broken-down minefield that hadn't seen public works in twenty years was a better use of the street than what they had now.

No, he didn't like that at all.

It was lead story on the evening news, went statewide, even landed a passing joke on a syndicated late-night show. The whole town was thrilled, the mayor excepted.

And the night after that Trev and I struck again, shock-and-awe style this time, dumping huge mounds of earth at the top of thirteen streets, with shovels, seeds, and instructions piled on top of them. People knew the deal now, we can't do it *all* for you.

We managed three more nights of that before we got

caught.

. . .

I was a first-time offender, at least as an adult, so even though the plan was mostly my idea I didn't get too harsh a sentence. When I got out, Trev still had a couple of years on his account. He didn't mind that so much, and certainly didn't blame me—as far as he's concerned, "Market Garden 2.0" was our most successful operation by far.

We both worked the prison farm, helped really make something of it. So when I headed back to the world I was leaving it in capable hands. Trev's developed a pretty green thumb. Said he had to, because the place needed someone reliable to keep things up to scratch until I got myself sent back in for the next big action.

That's not really part of my next plan, though.

See, those mountains of earth we left blocking streets all over town? Half of them are vegetable gardens now. The council doesn't like it and the mayor is *pissed*, but we mostly picked our targets well, and if there's one thing all politicians have long since learned it's that they can't afford to upset happy voters.

If there's one thing *I've* learned, it's this:

If you want to win the battle, choose the right battleground.

The fifth time I try to regreen my town, I'll be running for office.

ABOUT THE AUTHOR

Andrew Leon Hudson is a technical writer by day, and is technically a writer by night as well. He's an English genre author currently resident in Barcelona, Spain, where he's waiting for the world to end. His work has appeared in *Metaphorosis*, *Cossmass Infinities*, and *Triangulation: Dark Skies*, and he's coauthor of the naval fantasy-adventure novel *Archipelago*. You can find his links and other things at AndrewLeonHudson.wordpress.com, and anything else you've heard is speculation at best.

MOTHER NATURE

John Grey

SHE'S concerned,
fraught with worry even

and out of patience
with this constant
battering she takes

dead oceans,
melting glaciers,
mass extinctions,
pasture turned
to dust bowl or desert

her storms grow louder,
her hurricanes fiercer,
her tornadoes wilder

in anger yes
but mostly resignation

striking meteors she could accommodate
but she never saw evolution coming

doesn't understand
such overpowering self-centredness

for she's mother nature
not human nature

ABOUT THE AUTHOR

John Grey is an Australian poet and US resident, recently published in *Sin Fronteras, Dalhousie Review,* and *Qwerty* with work upcoming in *Blueline, Willard and Maple,* and *Red Coyote.*

THE HEAVENLY DREAMS
OF MECHANICAL TREES

Wendy Nikel

TREES were never intended to be sentient beings, or God
would have created them that way, back in the Garden.

Ailanthus ponders this sometimes as the sun's rays prickle
her leaves' tiny solar panels and the tubules of her stems
absorb the afternoon's deluge. If the Tree of Knowledge had
a voice, would it have cried out to warn the Tempted? Or
would it, too, have been deceived by the Serpent and the false
promises falling from its golden, forked tongue? Had it
spoken, might the Tree have saved its offspring? In a way, the
trees' first parents had failed them, too.

Though admittedly, Ailanthus is not a natural tree,
composed of wood and leaf and bark. No, she was created
by another hand, forged of copper and steel and gold, in a

factory not far from the Wind Forest. Its fumes are familiar to her. As soon as they're inhaled, they're processed through her leaves and exhaled again in a form fresh and renewed. The humans planted her here, her and her brethren—miles and miles of eight-armed trees-that-aren't-trees in a forest-that-isn't-a-forest. A second Eden, created to save the world.

Whether the other trees spend their days in philosophical ponderings, Ailanthus has no way to know. Though her branches scrape theirs when the wind blows just right and their roots are irreversibly entangled, their creators gave them no means by which to communicate, so their solidarity is one of silence. Thus, Ailanthus spends her days processing the air, dreaming her dreams, and wondering what she'd say if she had the words.

Something—no, *someone* stirs at the edge of the forest and Ailanthus shifts her attention from the skies, from the impossible flight of black-feathered birds and the way they pick the copper from her leaves' veins for their nests high in her cloud-closest branches.

• • •

"—with enough energy to power a hundred households for a hundred years in each and every tree."

"They're not trees." Bita's voice was hostile, accusatory. She knew how she sounded, but she didn't care. She hadn't wanted to come here anyway. The trees here cast eerie crisscrossed shadows and the wind whistling through their branches seemed a whisper of warning.

"*Bita.*" Aunt Gigi's disapproval manifested itself in

gradually deepening lines. Each wrinkle was unique: some longer, some thicker, some that oddly hooked themselves about along the contours of her face.

That, Bita thought, *is how a tree's branches ought to be.*

"Well, they're not trees," Bita said. "Not real ones, anyway. The real ones were each different. Complex and magnificent. Not like these things. These aren't even plants; they're machines—cold and hard and ugly."

"You know how long it took to build this wind forest? Decades upon decades. If it weren't for these trees and the others of their kind, Earth would be a wasteland—destroyed by years of pestilence and plague. You understand that, don't you?"

"Of course I do. I *am* a botanist."

"Botanist." Aunt Gigi snorted. "Why waste your time studying the things of the past? We need intelligent young people like you to continue the march of progress, to increase efficiency, to solve the problems of rusting roots and corroding xylem and phloem and ... and these birds! Shoo! Go away! Menaces, all of them, but they're endangered species now, so what can you do? There, doesn't that sound like a problem for a scientist to solve? How to keep them from picking apart our trees without driving them into extinction as well? Or better yet, figure out how to make these trees reproduce so we don't have to replace their rusting and broken parts every decade."

Bita had stopped to study one of the trees' eight identical branches. Sure, it carried out the chemical processes of a real tree—photosynthesis, respiration, transpiration—and even produced a "green" source of energy as a byproduct, but calling these mechanical structures "trees" was like calling a light bulb the sun.

"Please, Bita. At least consider it. We're terribly understaffed. We could use your help, and I know you could use the work."

Bita sighed and placed her hand on the nearest tree's trunk. Through the steel bark, she sensed the rushing fluids, the transference of energy pounding through the metal like a cold, mechanical heartbeat. And somehow, deep within the vibrations, somewhere among the hums and clicks and whirring of parts, Bita swore she heard a quiet voice say, "Please."

• • •

Ailanthus knows she's not long for this world. The harsh corrosion of her inner, movable parts produces friction and uncomfortable burns. The birds have stolen the copper from her uppermost leaves again this spring, yet not one of the trees' keepers have come around to replace them. Without these sun-nearest panels in optimal condition, she functions more slowly, barely eking out two-thirds of the energy she'd once produced each day.

The Creator once commanded the trees to reproduce: *the fruit tree yielding fruit after his kind, whose seed is in itself, upon the earth.* Perhaps His blessing is what the steel forest lacks. There was no booming, powerful "Let there be" as Ailanthus and her brethren rolled across the conveyer belt and down the assembly line, as branches were welded to trunks. There was no anointing of their roots as they were placed in the ground, no sprinkling of holy water on their leaves. Nothing but indifferent mechanical procedures and wearying nine-hour shifts and the afterthought, generations later, of fruit and seed and renewal and the bitter realization that what was once deemed the world's greatest solution was really no solution at all.

• • •

"I told you, Steve, they want me to do the impossible. They think a botanist is some sort of wizard, some sort of Dr. Frankenstein to bring dead objects to life." As she passed by each tree, Bita placed her palm on it, just long enough to hear the rumble of its inner workings. In the months she'd been working at the wind forest, she'd done this to each tree she passed but had never experienced that small, pleading voice again. Either she'd imagined it, or she was going crazy. Mama would've said it was a sign, a message from God, but Bita hadn't believed in that sort of thing for years, since her prayers for Mama's recovery had gone unanswered.

"These forests were supposed to solve the earth's problems," she said, frowning, "but we've only created more. The factories that manufacture new trees and replacement parts are using more energy than these worn-down acres can produce. They want me to make magic, to make these trees self-replicate like the trees of the old days used to."

"What if you had a seed?" Steve asked. "An acorn, or a piece of fruit, or pinecone? Could you do it then?"

Bita sighed. "If I had a seed? A real, viable seed? One that somehow, by some miracle, wasn't destroyed by the plague? Well, we wouldn't need these broken-down scraps of metal then, would we? It would take some time, but we could fill these rusted forests with living trees instead. Can you imagine? No more rust, no more clanking of branches when the wind blows, no more harsh glimmer of the afternoon sun reflecting off the metal panels. They say that the old trees used to have their own unique scents, that you could tell by just smelling whether you were in a forest of maple or cedar or pine. And the fruit—"

"We have fruit." Steve looked insulted, as though her words were a personal slight.

Bita laughed. "No, we don't. We have blobs of protein injected with artificial flavourings and synthetic vitamins."

"You're not going to be one of those mothers, are you?" He laughed as he took her hand.

"What do you mean?" It was Bita's turn to look insulted now.

"The kind who's obsessed with keeping her children from the evils of processed foods. Who'll spend a fortune on groceries to get real wheat and corn from halfway across the world."

"Who said I wanted to be a mother at all?"

• • •

Ailanthus wants nothing more than to be a mother. Nothing more than to give life. If she had the means, she would be her kind's Eve without a breeze-whisper's hesitation. *If* she had the means.

She's been listening to the young woman, watching her as the she tries to solve the forest's "sustainability problem," a problem Ailanthus equates with death. Not only her own—that she might bear bravely—but that of the forest itself.

Is there an afterlife for a forest of steel? A bright city of glory where branches won't rust, where their limbs won't snap in strong winds? And there, will they be reunited with those who've gone before? Their ancestors of fragrant wood and soft leaf?

• • •

"The numbers don't look good, Bita."

"Just six more months," she begged.

Not five years earlier, it was Aunt Gigi pleading for help, and now how the cogs had fully turned. Bita placed her hand on one trunk, then the next, searching for hope amid the rusting forest. Its rattling had grown so loud the women had to shout to be heard, but still Bita strained her ears, leaning in close, for some sign of that small, trusting voice.

"They're pulling our funding," Aunt Gigi said.

"Then I'll work without pay."

"We need to consider other viable options."

They both knew that there were no other *viable options*. Without the trees, the carbon dioxide levels would rise too quickly. Without the trees, everything would die.

"We need to start looking for solutions elsewhere," Aunt Gigi said.

Bita pressed her hand against another tree's trunk.

"Please ..."

And from somewhere deep within the clanking, clanging tree trunk, a single syllable emerged.

"Yes."

• • •

Ailanthus has never encountered the thing the woman calls a seed, but each day, she pushes her roots out farther, searching. The seams and joints creak as they unfurl the years' worth of gnarls and reverberate as they clash against those of her brethren.

The woman presses her hand to the metal trunk and speaks of a long-ago time, when in the place where they stand once stood a true forest, with branches eternally vibrant.

"Evergreens." The whispered word echoes through Ailanthus's branches, burrows deep in her soul.

Weeks pass. The woman wearies, resting her back against the trunk as she scribbles thoughts and ideas onto a plastic tablet, then shakes her head and erases them. The sweat on her brow is slick against the trunk's steel plating, but still, Ailanthus searches, calling upon her silent brethren for help.

Her roots extend, each tube stretched thin, breaking apart rock and ever searching. With the additional effort, she barely creates enough energy to keep her own processes functioning, much less power anything else. Around her, her brethren crumble and fall, carried away in beak-sized bits by the birds alighting on every branch, pecking and dismantling each leaf.

Lightning ignites the abandoned ruins, far on the forest's edge. Only the woman's swift call for help saves Ailanthus from the same fate.

Ashes to ashes, dust to dust.

• • •

The tree was dying. Its energy output was less than ten percent what it was just weeks ago. Still, Bita wouldn't give up. She shooed the birds from its branches and sheltered it from the rain, all while she sat in the shade of its branches and tried to devise a solution.

She soon ran out of spare parts to dull its rattling and materials to patch the rusted holes in its trunk. When a sparrow alighted upon it, it looked so natural a movement, Bita didn't even think to shoo it away until it had already tucked itself inside.

Perhaps that was what did it in, in the end.

Within moments of the bird's nesting within its trunk, the tree gave a jolt and a shudder, its branches extending one final time. The gears ground to a halt, and it let out a groan.

"Don't give up," Bita pleaded. "Look. Just look at what once was."

She held up the image on her tablet of a lush, green tree in the centre of a garden. *Quercus wislizeni*: the live oak.

The tree gave no sign of seeing.

• • •

Her limbs are immobile. Her gears are rusted stuck. Yet in that stillness comes a silence she's never experienced before. All her life has been filled with noise, the noise of mechanical parts clinking and clanking and shifting and moving. A noise she's associated with life.

But now, in the silence, she can hear those around her. Their dying thoughts fill her consciousness. The noise, the bustle, the wheels of progress which they'd so desperately tried to keep moving ... that was the thing disconnecting them.

In half-whispered thoughts, Ailanthus calls upon the others. She tells them what to look for, where they might find it. And then, she waits, saving her last reserves of energy.

• • •

Bita fell to her knees, head bent against the metal panels so corroded that she could almost, just almost imagine that it was the roughness of true bark. Her hand dropped to the ground beside her, and there she felt ... something.

There, protruding from the black soil, entwined in the mechanical tree's roots, was a block of amber. Within it was something she'd only seen in pictures of long ago: the battered, half-broken, yet undeniable form of an acorn.

• • •

Ailanthus's branches never rust. Her leaves are always bright. She looks down upon the cloud-swirled sphere, at the bright blotches of green.

Evergreen.

ABOUT THE AUTHOR

Wendy Nikel is a speculative fiction author with a degree in elementary education, a fondness for road trips, and a terrible habit of forgetting where she's left her cup of tea. Her short fiction has been published by *Analog, Nature: Futures, Podcastle*, and elsewhere. Her time travel novella series, beginning with *The Continuum*, is available from World Weaver Press. For more info, visit wendynikel.com.

FOR THOSE WHO WOULD COME AFTER

J. Bear McKenna

THE problem with Stella's dad had never been his stubbornness, even if that was why her mom divorced him. No, his problem had been entirely Newtonian: if anyone pushed him to get with the times, he had an equal and opposite reaction. When Stella's mom and brothers told him to upgrade the farm to be less of an environmental calamity, they might as well have been playing chicken with a tidal wave. On the other hand, when Stella pretended to take him on his own terms and just wrote some harmless emails about studying for her sustainable engineering degree ...

He still wouldn't change, but at least he wrote back.

"My grandfather grew up without A/C. I will not allow my grandkids go back to that kind of life."

"No microwave? How do they expect us to cook, start fires with two sticks?"

"I am NOT giving up my irrigation pump. I've got 380 acres of crops, like hell am I going to hand water them all."

But at the end of every email, he'd written, "Love, Dad."

And, in his will, he'd written, "To my daughter Stella I bequeath the farm in its entirety, with the certainty she will appreciate what's been built for her by those who came before."

Stella had wanted to sell the place as soon as she'd inherited it. It was falling apart, just like everything on Earth, and Stella planned to get a job on Mars once she graduated. However, after one look at the farmhouse's old-fashioned, electricity-sucking systems, she decided she couldn't let someone else keep running it the way it was. So she took a sabbatical and put what she'd learned to use.

First she had the HVAC hauled away and installed attic billows. They couldn't produce the same chill that air conditioning could, but they ventilated and cooled the farmhouse (no one needed a furnace anymore) enough to be comfortable. From then on, the farmhouse breathed with a soothing rhythm.

Next she tossed the microwave and built a solar oven under a skylight. Meals took hours to cook, but she could dump her ingredients inside and do something else for the rest of the day. While the solar oven cooked, it filled the house with mouth-watering smells.

Then she gave up the pump, which she replaced with a

gravity tub. The contraption of revolving cisterns moved water to the top of a tower, where it flowed through aqueducts to irrigate her crops more efficiently than any pump could.

For her finishing touch, she built a couple of wind turbines that drove the gravity tub, charged her tractors, ran electronics, and contributed to the power grid. Stella could have built more turbines and turned a profit on the electricity alone, but she waived her electrical fees. She had enough good fortune to spread around.

Her dad would have been pissed about the changes, especially her giving away electricity, but she made it up to him when she changed her mind about selling the place. She'd grow the same crops he had, but she'd grow them better.

Part of her suspected he'd appreciate what she'd built for those who would come after.

ABOUT THE AUTHOR

J. Bear McKenna lives in Maryland, USA with his wife (and sometimes editor), a dog, a cat, and a cockatiel, as well as an ever-growing hoard of books. His favourite stories are about following frail threads of hope through a world of sharp edges. When not writing sci-fi and fantasy, he spends his time cooking, running, and being a lawyer. He can be found on Twitter at @Jairbehr.

STORIES AND SECOND CHANCES

Tamoha Sengupta

RITHIKA'S home was now two-storeyed, but Baba lived there alone most of the time, ever since she had moved out because of her job. She wished that she could spend more time with her father, in their home. She knew how lonely Baba was, even though he always encouraged her to go and pursue her goals.

"Do something to help, Rithi," was what he always told her.

Now, as she stepped out of the auto and walked towards her home, she remembered her childhood, spent studying beneath the low-hanging bulb that lit their one-room house at night. She remembered her father coming back from work, sweaty and half-broken after a day of pulling rickshaws, but always with a smile on his tired face. Most of all, she remembered Baba's stories. The stories of where they belonged, of the home of their ancestors. Sunderbans. Meaning "beautiful forest" in Bengali.

• • •

Baba's first gift to her was a map. A map that had land where there were seas in the maps at school.

She had leaned closer, tracing the lines in the yellowed light.

"Baba, these places are not there in the maps at school!"

"Sunderbans." Baba's voice was quiet and haunted, and his fingers traced the paper over the land crisscrossed by rivers. "Before the mangroves disappeared, before the soil became too saline and the sea swallowed the land, that was where I lived."

Mangroves. Sunderbans. They were new words, and the next day Rithika had looked them up on the internet in the school computer.

They opened up a new world for her, a world that showed her the past in a way she'd never seen before. The unique structures of the trees. The way they grew in saline water, the way they protected the land against the sea and the cyclones. She read the articles about their disappearance, read in cold black letters the news of the submerging of the largest delta in the world. That day she'd learnt that she was a refugee in her own country—a climate refugee.

• • •

This evening, as father and daughter sat down on the rocking chairs on their balcony, Rithika felt a pang of sadness as she looked at Baba's weather-beaten face, at his sparse hair—now coloured silver.

His voice was rusty as he spoke.

"When do you go back?"

Rithika sighed. "In two days' time." She leaned forward, took a deep breath and said what she'd been wanting to say the whole day.

"Baba, I want you to come with me this time."

• • •

Kolkata—nicknamed "City of Joy"—was the city of Rithika's childhood before the flooding became more consistent, more permanent. Before it took longer for the waters to recede, and some areas remained permanently submerged.

"The waters have followed me," Baba used to say, trying to make light of the situation, but Rithika had read the worry and dread in his eyes.

Their house filled with water during the second consecutive year of the floods.

The two of them left the city, moving further inland, where the seas were no longer visible, where the air was no longer salty, where life was still a struggle.

The memories of the floods stayed with Rithika. She had wondered how much worse it must have been for Baba to see his home destroyed back when he was a young boy in the Sunderbans, to live with the knowledge that his childhood was forever submerged.

And that was when she knew what she was going to

become when she grew up.

• • •

It took some convincing for Baba to get into the helicopter, but he agreed eventually, his hands tightly clasped in Rithika's all the while.

She'd asked for permission to bring him as soon as she knew that she had to go for the inspection.

Now, they flew through the rain towards what had once been Kolkata. Most of the city lay submerged, and the parts that had survived were almost islands. College Street fought valiantly against the rising waters, its shops still full of books, although the shop owners had long abandoned the city. Rithika remembered frequenting the neighbourhood. She had fallen in love with this cramped place filled with noise and people and all the vibrant colours of endless books. The helipad was situated just a few metres away from the street now, and as they stepped outside the helicopter, Rithika saw that there were a few others already there for the inspection. She signalled to them that she'd be with them in a moment. She glanced back at her father, who was staring with wide eyes in front of him.

A few hundred metres away, the Bay of Bengal was visible, an expanse of rolling endless grey that merged with the sky.

Between the waters and College Street, rose rows and rows of endless trees.

Baba took a step forward. Cleared his throat.

"Are those—"

"Not the real ones, Baba." Rithika took a step forward too. She gently took hold of his hands and took a deep breath. "Remember the stories you used to tell me? About the trees of your childhood? We studied their structures. They're long gone, but we used them to build these artificial ones, with aerial and underwater roots that break the waves and all. We're working on improving them, trying to make them more efficient, so that they can also absorb floodwater—"

"Mangrove trees. My favourite was the *Sundari* tree." Baba's voice was dazed. "These trees—you built them yourself?"

"With the help of a few others." Rithika spoke through the sudden lump in her throat. "Right now, the plan is to plant these synthetic ones along coasts and low-lying lands —"

"We failed to save them." When Baba finally turned to look at Rithika, his eyes had filled with tears. In all her years, she'd never seen him cry. "They cut them down for wood and then there was nothing between us and the sea—"

She held him close as he wept. The years of loss, of painful memories seemed to surface and she let him pour it all out, her heart crying with him, this frail man who had carried her and supported her over the years.

"I cannot bring back those forests for you, Baba," she said, her voice trembling a little. "I wish I could, but I can only do so much."

"You are doing a lot, Rithi." He leaned back and smiled through his tears. "Doing something to help, right?"

She smiled back. "Doing something to help."

"And you'll always remember our stories and learn from them?"

"Always, Baba. And I'll tell them to others, through words and through these trees, so that they know as well."

• • •

And she did. As she travelled the world with her team, planting the artificial forest walls along coastlines, she told her stories just as she had promised her Baba. Because even though they hadn't protected the mangroves, the mangroves had come back to protect them.

And Rithika would always be grateful for that.

ABOUT THE AUTHOR

Tamoha Sengupta lives in India. She is a cyber security analyst by day and a speculative fiction writer at all other times. She enjoys watching anime, playing table tennis, or curling up with a good book. Her fiction has appeared in *Apparition Lit*, *Abyss & Apex*, *Daily Science Fiction*, and elsewhere. She sometimes tweets @sengupta_tamoha.

EXHIBIT E

L. P. Melling

PEOPLE first noticed it had changed on the turn of the full moon in October.

For the many who looked up at night, the moon appeared different somehow, but they could not put their finger on what had changed. Like a patient looking at an X-ray, the shading looked wrong, but they couldn't describe how without before-and-after images.

You needed a telescope to truly realize the change, and what you saw was beyond belief.

A giant replica of Earth was superimposed on the moon's lifeless grey surface: our planet reflected back at us.

Soon the internet was awash with satellite imagery and fevered discussion of the moon. Questions echoed around the world. Where was it being projected from? Why had it been created? What did it mean? A whole host of theories, conspiratorial and otherwise, sprung up. Talk show hosts riffed on the event and invited artists and scientists to discuss its value.

But that was just the start.

It was not a fixed image as people took it to be, but in movement like the thing it represented.

Night by night, it changed. Subtly at first, with the ice caps shrinking on the 3D copy of our planet. Then dramatically as landmasses disappeared before our eyes on live satellite feeds.

The oceans turned a deeper blue with a tint of blood red the following night, and entire continents burst into flame, smoke clouds drifting across half the planet.

Tsunamis swept across seas and oceans, leaving a trail of destruction and drowned islands in their wake. And if you magnified the image you could see other details. Belly-up whales and other sea life on the surface. Charred flora and trapped fauna.

The night after as the moon shrank further, barbed wire the size of stripped forests sprouted and wrapped itself around the globe. And the remaining few islands turned a dead grey, lifeless as the moon the image was displayed on.

And as the moon completed its cycle, the dead planet faded away to nothing. Like a Banksy piece, the priceless artwork was destroyed forever.

Afterwards, the world hailed it as the most ambitious art installation humanity had ever produced, and though it had countless critics, people began to wake up to its message.

No artist ever claimed credit for it, though many people claimed to know who had organised it. Clearly the piece was commissioned by someone with a hell of a lot of money, but it would remain as much a mystery as our own creation, as our self-destructive nature.

It was only later, when the Gemini Observatory scanned the projected image pixel by pixel that they found it. In an oil-spilled section of ocean floated a raft of plastic bottles arranged to spell the artwork's title: *Exhibit E.*

The signature took people time to make out, the scrawl illegible, until a team of handwriting experts deciphered it: *H. Nature.*

Now people continue to look up at the moon's illumination, wondering if the image will return, and they do more than ever to stop it from becoming reality.

ABOUT THE AUTHOR

L. P. Melling currently writes from the East of England, UK, after academia and a legal career took him around the country. His fiction has appeared in such places as *Typehouse*, *DreamForge*, and the Best of Anthology *The Future Looms*. When not writing, he works for a legal charity in London that advises and supports victims of crime. He is 50% herbal tea drinker, 100% recyclable. You can find out more about him at www.lpmelling.wordpress.com.

URGENT CARE

Mark S. Bailen

NELLI Song sniffled as she entered the low-gravity waiting room. The room was filled with various species from the Orion Arm, most of them related to the Hant Collective, three-headed beings who talked with their feet. She shuffled towards the window. Her hair was in a bun and she wore grey sweatpants, a college sweatshirt, an air filter, and Converse All Stars. An Orileon Stomper pushed out a clipboard with papers to fill out.

"Translator, please," Nelli mumbled.

The Stomper stared for a moment before lifting a black metal box and pointing to it.

Nelli leaned towards the metal box. "I need a translator."

The Stomper whistled and a short Fuscillian Bont waddled around the desk and led Nelli to the back of the waiting room, dragging along a small console. The pair settled into two big purple molded chairs. The Bont had stubby limbs and wore a mask. "What brings you here today?"

"My planet," Nelli said.

"Not feeling well?"

"No."

"I'm sorry to hear that." The Bont had a low droning voice. "Name of planet?"

"Earth."

"Type?"

"Terrestrial."

"Size?"

"Average, I think."

"And how much does your planet weigh?"

"Weigh?" Nelli frowned. "Oh, I'm not sure."

"We can figure that out later. Atmosphere?"

"Nitrogen mostly. With some oxygen."

"Average temperature?"

"Fifty to sixty degrees ... Fahrenheit."

"Any temperature spikes? Chills?"

"Well, things do seem to be getting warmer."

"Warmer? How much warmer?"

"A few degrees."

The Bont paused. Its ears twitched and then it pressed some buttons on its console. "Any radiation? Surface scarring? Dead zones?"

"No."

"Decline in your water cycle?"

"Not that I know of."

"Excess gas?"

"No."

"Increase in traumatic weather?"

"Maybe."

"Loss of ecological diversity?"

"Yes."

The Bont wiggled its fingers. "And what's your major complaint today?"

"Climate change."

The Bont nodded severely. "Anything else?"

Nelli shook her head.

The Bont pressed more buttons. "Just a few more questions for billing. What species are you?"

"Human."

"Honzis, haroocroo, hamsters ... human. There you are. Do you speak for the entire planet?"

"Me?"

"No, humans. Do humans speak for the entire planet?"

"Sort of."

"Sort of?"

"Well, Earth does have a lot of species. But humans tend to take charge. And humans are self-aware. Some of us feel bad, maybe even responsible for our planet's climate change."

"I'll just put 'yes.' " The Bont tapped the screen. "And do you have insurance?"

"Insurance?"

"A GPO, an SMO, or something from the galactic exchange?"

Nelli shifted in her seat. "No."

"That's fine. We'll figure out payment later." The Bont hopped off its chair. "Wait right here for your planet to be called. The doctor will see you soon."

• • •

In twenty minutes, Nelli was ushered into a small white room with various types of exam tables. On the wall hung educational posters about maintaining the health of your planet. The posters were printed in polyglot blocks, which she could barely decipher. One said, "Solar Flares and You." Another said, "Know Your Magnetic Field." A third, "You and Comet-Transmitted Diseases."

While waiting, Nelli paced the small room, questioning why she had come all this way for urgent care. Her family thought she was being a worrywart. Her coworkers called her overly dramatic. Her best friend proclaimed that going into space was a waste of resources, resources that could be better spent on Earth. But Nelli needed to know. She yearned for an outsider's opinion. She wanted to hear from an expert that Earth was OK.

• • •

Finally the doctor arrived. It was a Pex Jah Loofin with multiple arms, periwinkle skin, and a white coat. It was followed by the Bont. The doctor made a number of wheezing noises that the Bont quickly translated.

"Good morning, Nelli. Oh my, you look terrible. Is your planet not treating you well?" The doctor eyed the console and then snapped three hands. "No, no. Forget that. You're a human. That's how you're supposed to look." It tilted its head. "So what seems to be the problem?"

Nelli sat on an exam table and took a long breath. "Climate change."

The Bont translated.

The doctor cocked its head the other way. "And on a scale of one to ten, how bad is it?"

"Um." Nelli fidgeted. "Some people think it's a ten and Earth is doomed. Others think it's a one, and no big deal."

"Just give me a number."

"Three." Nelli shook her head. "No, seven."

"Let's call it a five." The doctor wheezed. "What do you hope to accomplish today?"

"I want to make sure that Earth is OK."

The doctor made an expression that could have been a smile. "That seems like a reasonable request. I think we can do that." The doctor went over to the sink and washed its hands. "How are things since you left? It's not apocalyptic is it?"

"Not quite."

"But also, not paradise?"

"Right."

"Is your sun producing enough heat?"

"Yes."

"Is your atmosphere still intact?"

"Yes."

"Wonderful. Let's take a closer look." The doctor tapped on the console and a large hologram of Earth popped up in the middle of the room. "These images are from four months ago, but they should give us a good sense of what's going on." The hologram rotated and zoomed. The doctor stood back and waved its four arms. "What a beautiful planet. Nice cloud coverage. Large oceans. Teeming with life. You have a vibrant magnetic field."

"Thank you." Nelli felt slightly proud.

The doctor fiddled with the hologram, seeming to feel for a pulse. "And the temperature looks fine. Perfect for water-based lifeforms. Although there are signs of warming."

Nelli's stomach dropped. "There are?"

"It's not critical. Not yet." The doctor wheezed. "But I do see evidence of rising sea levels. Melting ice caps. And maybe an increase in cataclysmic storms?"

"I know."

"Has your planet experienced this before?"

"Not that I know of."

"How far back does your climate history go?"

She stammered.

"Did you bring records?"

The Bont interrupted. "Earth's records have been transferred to the database."

"Wonderful." The doctor turned back to the console and made a humming noise. "The data's a little spotty. Not much prior to ten thousand years. But I do see evidence of climate change. The fluctuations are fairly regular. Earth's gone through more than a few ice ages. And a number of extinction events. Both rising and falling ocean levels. It looks like a chronic issue."

Nelli lowered her head.

"Don't fret. It's a normal diagnosis for a terrestrial planet of your size. Especially one that's nontidally locked and has large oceans. We see it all the time."

"You do?"

"Sure." The doctor folded its four arms. "And as a dominant species, there are things you can do. Nobody likes unpredictable weather, do they? Or major extinction events. If your species can control its risky behaviour, you'll get through this. Everything will be fine."

"Really?"

"Really." The doctor patted her on the knee and went back to the console. "I'm going to prescribe you some global-biotics that should help with species loss. I also suggest cutting down on greenhouse gases, stopping nuclear weapons proliferation, and placing caps on your pollution. Understand?"

"Yes."

"You can fill this at the pharmacy." He handed her a prescription. "Is there anything else?"

"Huh?"

"Do you have any more questions?"

Nelli tried to think. She had travelled halfway across the galaxy and felt strangely unsatisfied. The appointment had lasted less than five minutes. She hadn't even considered asking another question. "I don't think so," she said.

"Fine." The doctor turned towards the door. "It was nice

meeting you. Have a pleasant trip back to your home planet."

The Bont waddled past.

"Wait." Nelli jumped off the table. "Just to make sure, Earth will be fine, right? That's what you are saying?"

"Of course." The doctor turned. "Your planet is perfectly healthy. And it should remain so for at least a hundred million years."

"A hundred million! Oh, thank god!" Nelli released her breath and clasped her hands. "It's such a relief."

"I'm glad."

She stepped back. "And our species? We will be fine too?"

The doctor paused. "What's that?"

The air vents moaned.

The Bont looked at the floor.

"Our species. Humans," said Nelli. "Will humans be OK too? Will we also survive for a hundred million years?"

The Bont twitched its ears.

The doctor folded its arms. "I'm sorry, but I can't answer that."

"You can't?"

"No." The doctor wheezed. "For that, you need a specialist."

ABOUT THE AUTHOR

Mark S. Bailen is an author, illustrator, website developer and lousy photographer. He lives in an orange cabin in the woods in Flagstaff, AZ with his wife and teenage son. He has published in the *High Plains Literary Review*, the *Sonora Review* and the *Cimarron Review*. He has also written and illustrated an award winning children's book about the environment, titled *Earf*.

AN APOLOGY FROM THE NATIVES OF EARTH

Jon Lasser

WE'RE sorry. We didn't mean to make such a mess of things.

It all started around a hundred thousand years ago. We'd only just evolved into our modern form and begun to spread from our cradle in East Africa. Down in Australia we wiped out *diprotodon optatum*—a two-ton wombat, more or less—as fast as we could throw our spears. Knocked out the giant kangaroos too, and the thunder birds, and far more species than I have time to recount in this apology. We did the same elsewhere, too, chasing the mammoths over the land bridge into the Americas, where we hunted every last one of them down.

It was different then, you understand. I'm not making excuses, but we weren't talking to one another. We had no written language, no higher mathematics. No way could we conduct a survey, jot down some quick treaties, and hunt within our quotas. We hadn't evolved enough culturally, and once the ball got rolling—well, it was another fifty thousand years and we couldn't keep from killing ourselves with pea soupers in The Old Smoke. If we weren't dying in that toxic London fog, it was only because we were too busy watering our lawns with the Colorado River until it couldn't reach the sea. It wasn't hard to know we'd overshot, that the land couldn't sustain all of us in good health, but we couldn't coordinate a response.

It wasn't just the coal smoke from heating homes. It was deforestation. Desertification. The motorcar. Radioactive fallout from The Bomb. Waste from nuclear reactors. Overfishing. Pesticides. The Pacific Garbage Patch. Genetically-engineered diseases. Nanobots turning a handful of our own cities into grey-goo swamps. Each one of those deserves to be an apology unto itself. And it happened so fast that we couldn't make sense of it.

The climate crisis was the worst of our messes. I've mentioned the motorcar, but not the sprawl it created. The mechanized destruction of habitats at a scale unimaginable since the earliest stirrings of agriculture. And the runaway atmospheric reaction, freeing methane from the permafrost, melting the polar ice caps and raising ocean levels. We couldn't organize ourselves to stop it, not with half the planet shouting, "Everything is fine, it's not even happening." Worse, our entire economic system's fundamental premise was that wealth emerged from resource extraction. Can you believe it? But promise someone a meal and they'll shovel themselves into the furnace of progress like so much strip-mined coal.

It's said that every intelligent species comes to a moment where they risk overshooting the carrying capacity of their homeworld, that most species experience a sort of cultural adolescence when they fail to clean up after their messes. Each is a little bit different, but there's a generalized shape, and a reckoning. Some planets figure it out. Others don't. But almost every one walks right up to the brink of the abyss and stares deep into it. Like everyone else, we'd figured we'd die choking on our own filth.

Then we cleaned it up. One hundred years from the first photograph of Earth as seen from outer space to save our skins. We couldn't set it right, not all of it, but we stopped the worst of it. We cleaned the air. We repopulated the oceans. We solved the disposal of nuclear waste and nanoparticulates alike. And we did it ourselves, without any help from you, whom we hadn't yet met.

We were nearly done cleaning up when the signs you'd left us came clear. There, in skies cleansed of toxic waste, we read your message. Your invitation. And we walked through the door you left for us, right into—everywhere else.

All the pressure was off. You understand? We'd had only a hundred years of good behaviour. It wasn't quick by the scale of human lives, but in an evolutionary sense we were the same myopic hunters who'd chased mammoths across the Bering Land Bridge and gorged ourselves on their flesh until we could eat no more. Now we had a thousand worlds or more to spread across, planets scattered across the whole Orion-Cygnus Arm, each a buffet of untapped ecosystems, and we wanted to taste them all.

That's what this latest mix-up has been about. The destruction of all six intelligent species on Pok-mok-Nahat (what we on Earth used to call Epsilon Eridani V) was a terrible thing, but it's been tough adapting to our new reality. I'm sure you remember what it was like. So, yes, there's been some backsliding. What else can we say besides how sorry we are? We mean that most sincerely.

Despite these small slips lately, we've grown up. I promise. There's absolutely no need to proactively vaporize us, we'll clean up Tau Ceti e, and all the other planets where we've made our home, just like we've cleaned up Earth. We have a track record. You can count on us.

ABOUT THE AUTHOR

Jon Lasser was born in New York City. He lives and writes in Seattle, WA.

He is a graduate of the Clarion West writers' workshop. His stories have appeared or are forthcoming in *Diabolical Plots*, *Galaxy's Edge*, *Untethered: A Magic iPhone Anthology*, and elsewhere.

When not writing or working in the tech industry, Jon spends time with his wife and children, cooks, and scuba dives. He prefers cold-water over tropical diving.

WHEN LAST THE CICADAS SANG

Anthony W. Eichenlaub

"LET'S go listen for cicadas," Ansibel said. The eight-year-old picked at a big book of insects with grubby fingernails. "They should come out soon."

Kara stood, stretching her old back. Weeding the garden next to her farmhouse had always been a way to relax after a long day, but it got harder and harder every year. And now this. Kara knew better than to fight her granddaughter's foolish optimism head-on. The child wouldn't believe anything but the shiniest rays of hope, and Kara had run clean out of those ages ago. "We can walk out and see," she said. Truth was, she needed to walk her fields from time to time anyway.

"Cicadas can live underground for a long time," Ansibel

said, paging through her book. Big, glossy photos of the periodical insects filled whole pages. "Then they all come out at once."

It served Kara right for letting the kid read the old stack of children's books from the farmhouse basement. She'd be hearing about cicadas for a week before something else sparked the kid's interest.

Gravel crunched underfoot as the two left the farmhouse and made their way toward the setting sun. Late spring winds carried away the damp scent of melted snow, and birds danced along the pine windbreak along the long driveway.

They followed a trail into the field, where the freshly seeded soybeans grew up alongside stocky hazelnuts. This was Kara's oldest hazelnut field, established after a corn and soy rotation had nearly ruined the soil. Now, the earth was rich and deep, and Kara bent down to run her fingers through it.

"The book says they like to sing," Ansibel said. "At dusk."

"It's been a long time since anyone's heard the cicadas sing, dear."

"Why?"

A knot formed in the back of Kara's chest. "A long time ago, scientists warned of a disaster, and folks didn't believe them. They said there'd be a change in temperature. They said our soil would die."

They walked in silence for a long time, but the words stuck in Kara's throat. It had been so long since she'd spoken of any of this. The last dregs of the sunset's orange glow set the pines alight as the two passed the barrier forest. The field beyond was fallow, long since returned to its original wetland in an attempt to bring peace to the ravaged earth. Beyond, the first few fireflies of the evening sparked in the shadows. They had survived, at least.

Finally, Ansibel said, "We learned about the big climate change in school. It got bad and then you fixed it."

"It wasn't me who fixed it," Kara said.

"But you helped. You were a farmer, weren't you?"

"Yes," Kara said. "I was."

"In class we learned that the farmers helped stop climate change by changing what they planted and by changing how they used soil." The book closed in Ansibel's hands, and she gripped it tightly.

What could Kara tell the child? The truth hurt so much. Still, truth was all she could think to say. "I wasn't a hero, Ansibel. I denied the changes even as the world burned and the oceans turned to acid. The storms came and we fought so hard because changing our way of life seemed too painful. Too threatening."

"But weren't the storms more threatening?"

"Sometimes nothing is as scary as admitting you're wrong."

"Oh." The girl's response couldn't possibly have carried all the accusation Kara felt she deserved, but it was close.

Guilt ached cold in Kara's chest like shards of a broken icicle. "We eventually changed when the laws made us change, but it was too late. It didn't fix things fast enough because of folks like me," Kara said. "The world returned to something like normal, but by then a lot of animals were gone. We almost lost the bees. Took a while before they realized all the cicadas were gone."

The eight-year-old's brow furrowed. Not only were the cicadas gone, but to discover the person responsible for their passing was her own grandmother? The child would never hear their beautiful song. Never! Kara couldn't imagine how much that must hurt.

Then, Ansibel said, "Maybe they aren't all dead. Maybe they're only being quiet."

"The cicadas?"

"My book says they're not always noisy. And it says sometimes they stay underground for years and years."

"It's been—" but the words choked in Kara's throat. She sat on a fallen log. Some oak felled years ago on the farm. Ansibel sat next to her. What more could she tell the girl? How could she admit to Ansibel that there really was no more hope? It had been fifty years since anyone had heard a cicada. "Let's listen for a while, then," she said.

Together, they sat watching the lightning bugs dance across the fallow wetlands, and when Kara listened at the very edge of hearing, she heard the far-off song of the cicadas echoing to her from across those many, many years.

ABOUT THE AUTHOR

Anthony W. Eichenlaub is the author of short stories featured in *Curious Fictions* and the anthologies *A Punk Rock Future* and *Fell Beasts and Fair*. His science fiction novels aim for the lofty goal of "serious ideas, absurdly fun", and vary from the Minnesotan technothriller *Grandfather Anonymous* to the planet-crashing adventure *Of a Strange World Made*. In his spare time he enjoys woodworking, landscaping, and macro photography.

ENCROACHMENT

Floris M. Kleijne

THE couch in the experimental botany lab is too short even for me. I sit up with a groan, the tinfoil emergency blanket crumpling in my lap, scattering the light from the overhead fluorescents. I stretch my arms above my head in a vain attempt to get my back in working order. Time was, I could sleep here without wrecking my spine. I wish I could blame the higher gravity, like I wish it had been Joel's snoring that had driven me from our bed last night, the snoring I can just hear over the hum of the power cells.

Time was, I would bear the buzz-saw ruckus from his throat just for the joy of spooning.

As I rub the sleep from my eyes, I try to remember what started the fight this time. All that comes back to me is shouting at the top of our voices, in counterpoint, Joel's rough rumbling bass and my own high-pitched scream. I cringe with embarrassment.

I glance at the terrariums crowding the lab floor, but choose not to look closer. I don't feel up to the task yet of taking stock of our experiments. If the pattern holds, the grey decay will have advanced again during the night.

Fatigue overwhelms me, and I slump back, pressing my hands against my face as I squeeze my eyes closed, refusing my tears an exit. It must have looked great on paper, sending out scientist couples to investigate the viability of exoplanet colonies. We called our assignment on Kapteyn b our second honeymoon among the stars. The perfect couple: Joel, the exobiology/physics double PhD, and me, Olivia, the botanist/engineer.

Only thing is, they forgot to include a marriage counselor.

• • •

Through the lab window, in Kap's depressing pale red light, I see that the gritty grey darkness of the local soil has claimed three more rows of corn overnight. About forty feet out, leaves and stalks form an amorphous dike of decay around our module. If the same has happened in all directions again, we now have fewer than two acres of arable land left.

At this rate, we'll have no land at all by the end of next week.

"Joel!" I holler.

Succumbing to my desperate desire for routine and normalcy, I check the terrariums after all, and record my findings. Strawberries: eighty percent overtaken by the grey decay. Potatoes: eighty-five percent. Cassava: sixty-nine.

"Joel!"

I do the math in my head. The extraction shuttle will take two weeks to get here. Our frozen supplies will easily support us that long. But two weeks means the grey decay may have swallowed our entire plot before we're extracted. We have no idea what will happen when we run out of space. Will the module withstand the assault? Or will it crumble into a sagging, colourless ghost of itself, like the crops?

Will we?

"Joel! Get your ass out of bed right now!"

Finally, I hear noises from our living quarters. Stumbling feet, running water, the harsh grind of the coffee maker. The smell of fresh coffee precedes my husband into the lab. The smell of hangover follows him.

"What!"

I process our ever more frequent fights through short nights and long work. He takes his medicine.

He is carrying a single, steaming mug. In some alternate universe, it would have been for me. A pang of pain rips through my heart when I realize that this alternate universe is only a month in our past. He hasn't bothered to get dressed; his hairy legs stick out under his robe. I take a deep breath, which does precious little to calm my irritation.

"Forty feet left."

"Shit," he says.

• • •

All day, we go through the motions, working the fields, teasing life out of our crispered crops, hoeing the strange weeds out of what's left of the purple-green soil, performing our measurements. By unspoken agreement, we're granting ourselves a few hours of hope, though I'm not sure myself what I'm hoping for. We both know we'll send the extraction call tonight.

Dinner is silence and thawed soup.

"Olivia?" he says as we clear the table. I glance at him and make a noncommittal sound.

"I'm still glad we tried. And they can't all be successes, right? That's why they're called seed colonies."

My hands full of cutlery and food wrapping, I stop and turn to Joel. He stands facing me, hands spread at his sides, shoulders raised in a half shrug. He wears a slight, wistful smile, but his eyes are brimming. As olive branches go, this is a huge one for him.

"Oh Joel," I sigh, and step into his hug.

• • •

The extraction protocol app waits for our input. I enter my authorization code. Joel adds his own five digits. He's quick, but I notice that he's chosen my birthday as his code.

He lifts his hand to tap the Extract button.

"Are you sure?"

Gently, I take his wrist. I begin to speak without knowing what I'm about to say.

"What happened to us, Joel? We were happy when we came here, weren't we?"

He winces, and I hold my breath. But the defensive lash-out I fear doesn't come.

"We were. And we will be again, Livvy."

I can't remember when he last called me that. He places his hand against my cheek. I kiss it and slide my chair closer to his. Our arms, our mouths rediscover the familiar paths. Trailing discarded clothes, we make our way to the bedroom.

Barely.

• • •

We greet the next morning with an endless kiss. Stepping out of bed naked and smiling, Joel says, "Coffee?" and disappears into the kitchen. Instead of the coffee maker, there's silence.

"Joel?"

"You'd better come see for yourself."

In the kitchen, Joel stands motionless, staring out at the potato field. I slide my arms around him and look over his shoulder.

It takes a moment to sink in. The outermost ring is still bare of plants, but its colour has returned, no longer the grey of decay, but the purple-green of Kap's healthy soil. My hands randomly explore Joel's body as I try to remember. Was our unhappiness caused by the increasing difficulties? Did our fighting result from the encroaching grey decay?

Or had it been the other way around?

"Only one way to find out," I whisper in Joel's ear, and softly bite his lobe.

ABOUT THE AUTHOR

Floris M. Kleijne is the author of over three dozen short stories in *Daily Science Fiction*, *Galaxy's Edge*, *Factor Four*, and numerous other publications. He lives in a 200-year-old house in the Dutch river district, but does most of his writing on trains. Floris was the first Dutchman to win the prestigious *Writers of the Future* contest, as well as the first Dutchman to qualify for active membership of the SFWA. He blogs about writing, Real Life™, and atrocious customer service on www.floriskleijne.com, where you can also read more of his stories.

LITTLE GOATS

Clio Velentza

OLD Man Proteus thought that land was overrated, yet he crawled out onto the shore, shook off the brine, and changed into his old-man form because land was where his business lay. He wasn't very fond of the sameness of things that he passed by: people seemed drawn to the concept of uniformity and celebrated its elementary, comforting power. Old Man Proteus liked it best when everything was misshapen and oozy, like himself.

Old Man Proteus stayed for a while in the dripping bungalows of the resorts, the best place to keep his beard mossy and his feet cool, and pondered where to begin his search. He cursed his foundling water-spirits and their antics for making him drag his aching body out here, for making him abandon the tangy water that was his lifeblood and go out to look for them.

Ah, but the water-spirits, he thought, their bright, mercurial tempers and their jealous fits. They were so new to him, mere children, and would not be contained. He might as well have tended—well, not sheep, but a herd of vengeful storm clouds. And yet here he was, growing soft in his old age, out to shepherd them back home. As homeless spirits do, they yearned to settle into a body, those preposterous things.

Old Man Proteus shook his head. *Settling* for these spirits meant havoc. They longed to whirl through human minds and drive them to madness, the unusual taste of which they craved so often, and so rarely found in the void-black pastures of his well-tended abysses. This is what happens when you've been trapped in *ice* for most of the ages of the world, he mused, and coughed.

Old Man Proteus did not mind *ice*, but he was terribly proud of his velvety, lightless gorges and the tender violence of their blind inhabitants. But these spirits were misfits and wanted change. He picked irritably at his loose scales. If he could gift them his shapeshifting power, he would; all he ever used it for nowadays was minding his seaweed kingdoms. These spirits usually made their mischief, got bored of it, and soon were back. But not now. Now they had gone too far. Now he had to *walk*, he had to *cough* in the arid island air, he had to gurgle out words and ask the island folk whether they had—*cough, gurgle*—seen any wet and unusual phenomena. He wondered, did sheep ever behave like that? No, not sheep—goats perhaps, but that was land-business and beyond him.

A fishmonger took a liking to him and his gentle ways

with the lolling lobsters in her basket, and she told him that a group of peculiar young women had been the talk of the town. They had a funny air about them, she said, a sort of limpness of bearing, as if they had been flowers overcome by heat. They had dark translucent eyes, a favourite among the local lads. Several of these lads had followed them and hadn't been seen since. Old Man Proteus thanked her, scratched a lobster's wagging tail and walked on, leaving chilly pools of brackish water.

Why would the water-spirits behave so? He considered the warm days when they had first floated into his kingdom, newly released from their prison, like so many effervescent tricks of light: how happy and docile they had been.

They were slow to know him, slow to understand the order of his creatures and saltwater realm. They were used to a crystalline kind of life and couldn't adapt to his premeditated kind of chaos. They were set free haphazardly like wildlings, and no sea could contain their restless hearts.

This time he would have to make sure: they couldn't go running from him again. He'd have to do something final, keep them close forever. Old Man Proteus scratched his coral-crusted chest as if it ached him at the thought.

He reached the outskirts of a town and spied the low structure of a gas station. How could people stand this *dust*, this unbearable *dryness*? It grew worse every time. His insides constricted and pain throbbed behind his ears. My goats, he thought in a brief moment of delirium, I have to find my beautiful, thawed-out goats and take them home.

Home. His home, not theirs. Their home had melted rapidly in deafening snaps and falls, releasing puffs of methane and its carefree spirit inhabitants to the care of his gnarled hands.

Old Man Proteus squinted, parting the curtain of his eyebrows, and saw human-like shapes gathering in the gas station. It was a hot summer afternoon, and the street was empty and quiet. A dog barked somewhere far away and the air shimmered. There was a car parked at the station. The pump was still hooked on it, spilling its oily contents onto the ground. The shapes were gathered over a figure fallen on the concrete. Girl shapes. When they saw Old Man Proteus they laughed and sparkled.

My little goats, he thought tenderly. There's no place for them anymore.

The driver lay sprawled, his skin blotchy, white and blue. Old Man Proteus was used to seeing people like this: pale and immobile, drifting quietly while sea critters nibbled at them. But here, in this relentless heat—it was all *wrong*. Icy water ran out of the drowned man's mouth. Old Man Proteus looked at the girls. Water dripped from all their pockets. They tried to hide it but it ran through their fingers.

"Come on, my little ones," he said.

He opened his arms and the girls, laughing, crowded against him. He smelled the good smells on them: seawater, permafrost, salt. They would come back, but they would always run away.

"Come, my little goats."

His closed his arms around them and the girls giggled and squeezed together. The arms grew, no longer man-limbs but the supple appendages of a kind, elderly leviathan of the deep trenches.

The girls gasped and tried to squirm free, but they struggled in vain. One after another their spines snapped. Their luminous skin came loose and water gushed out, washing away the dirt, the gasoline. In the hazy light they erupted like handfuls of foam, sending swarms of rainbows dancing around.

The flow of water lessened to a trickle. They were gone and there was only an old man now, standing alone; bent and exhausted, in wet, ragged clothes. His cupped hands still held on to something.

Carefully he opened them and looked in. Tiny golden flames quivered timidly in his palm, hovering as if about to blow away. The delayed echo of laughter burst out of them and then was gone.

"Come here, my loves ..."

One by one he lapped them up. They sizzled and sighed as they dissolved in the salty cavern of his mouth.

"My little goats ..."

The heat was stifling. Old Man Proteus wiped his mouth and then his eyes, and turned to begin his long way home.

ABOUT THE AUTHOR

Clio Velentza is a writer from Athens, Greece. She is a winner of Best Microfiction 2020, Wigleaf's Top 50 2019 and The Best Small Fictions 2016, and a Pushcart Prize nominee. She writes prose and plays, and her work has appeared or is forthcoming in several literary journals, such as *Fractured Literary*, *The Arcanist*, *Jellyfish Review*, *The Journal of Compressed Creative Arts*, and *Wigleaf*. You can find her on Twitter at @clio_v.

NEW SNOW

Christopher Mark Rose

DON'T ever forget
what winter used to be
that peregrine dog
a shy prancer who
would lie down in the street
showing his white fluffy belly

I love crunchy silences, the fleeting
sculptures of exhaled breath, the
elegant oaks in their ghost crowns,
refracting the rough blinter of stars

I remember pulling joy,
a warped sled on a frozen rope,
across the forest landscape, we go
out where chandeliers dance

Your naked hand shaking
fingers wet and red
heaving a cold comet
your laughter a wind chime

Don't ask me again how long
freeze your belief into a simple formula
we see the truth written
we live with the hope
that the great soft machines will come soon—
drifting silent, languid,
lying down in the updrafts
letting sunbeams scratch their bellies
carbon-breathing
purifying
revising the sky.

Haunt me always
your white dress hung on naked sumac
for now I will carry
an acorn, a star, a mitten, a rope.

ABOUT THE AUTHOR

Christopher Mark Rose is a husband and father, an electrical engineer for NASA spacecraft, and in his spare time an author of speculative fictions. His writings have appeared in *Interzone*, and *Dreamforge*, and are forthcoming in *Asimov's* and *UNCANNY*. He attended the most recent Viable Paradise writers' workshop, and is founder for the Charm City Spec reading series. He hopes his stories are affecting, humane, and concerned with large questions.

FIELD TRIP

L. X. Beckett

A body is only as healthy as its weakest link, my grandma says, but when I look at Duck Sink and then I port into a class in Saskatoon or one of the other big cities ... well, I dunno. Saskatoon looks pretty healthy to me. It has topsoil cooperatives and VR production companies. If you don't like your neighbourhood's food rules or the bus routes, you can shop the options. Walk to a new part of the city, and set up house.

But Duck Sink's OK, I guess, at least when people aren't meeting endlessly about the impacts of eating machine-grown meat, or trying to get the greenhouses diversified so our fresh component gets to be something other than carrots and turnips. The water's clean and sweet and the skies are thick with waterfowl: geese, swans, coots, and the ducks that give the region its name. Each morning before school, we gather to meditate and take the measure of the air. Wet or dry, cold or warm, west or east wind, sweet or sour. We scent for hay and notes of the forest we're planting north of the town, in the wildfire-scorched deadlands.

A whiff of skunk yesterday made everyone laugh, but that poke to the nose, our teacher says, means that rewilding is getting traction. A bigger range of animals is coming back into the North. We've been hosting a travelling woods whisperer, an old woman and her apprentices, who walked here all the way from Edmonton. They came in person, if you can believe. Just in time to congratulate us all on that wafting stink!

There's no reek of skunk this morning as we group up, all the ten- to fourteen-year-olds from Duck Sink. It's warm enough to ride to the regional polling station and our teacher, Chris, is handing out bikes, vintage recycled frames fitted for new tires. Kezia gets a booster battery for her chair; she'll take point.

My heads-up display shows the route to the polls and a warning about a new pothole on the crosstown trail.

"Fezzi! Hey, Fezz." Mico's been self-isolating for three weeks. His mother claims it was just an allergic reaction to printed kidney meat, but the quarantine officer doesn't screw around these days. You pop a fever, your whole family goes into lockdown. Me, I think he just worked up a case of fake sniffles after Xi turned him down for a date. "Fezzi, hey, what's class today?"

"You got the daily digest, didn't you?"

"Come on, don't make me load that thing."

Gran would have lots to say about me chewing Mico's homework for him, but I'm a you-do-you type. He's trickster grade, you know? Charming the birds from the trees, like the song says. Maybe one day he'll be mayor. Maybe one day he'll smooth-talk a new plant for Duck Sink. If there was more factory work here, I might forget Saskatoon.

"It's a field trip, stupid," I tell him.

Eyeroll. "Obviously."

"We get to vote."

"Vote on what? Come on, Fezz."

I'm about to answer when the teachers wrangle us onto the road, Kezia in the lead, teachers in the rear to make sure nobody straggles.

I love it when we break out the bikes. I get to choose an International Giving option next fall, and I'm thinking about working on bicycle reclamation for communities with bad transport. It's trickier than it sounds. If village roads are bad enough, the bikes need smart tires instead of plastiprint, which means more of a resource draw. Harder to get the donations raised, harder to get the carbon cost of manufacture green-lighted. Longer queues for the production factories.

But the bragging rights, if we get smartwheel bikes shipped somewhere they're really needed? Even Gran says it'd look good on my college applications.

I didn't use to look at the roads as I rode over them, didn't think about how the land beneath you could pull you back, add to your base friction. Now I'm thinking about bike affordances, I see every stretch of smooth pavement, every desire line ... and every chunk of recycled asphalt breaking up the texture. Kezia's chair has smart tires and it's like she's flying as we all push uphill, up down, up down. I have to stand on the pedals before we crest the hill.

"Fezz, vote on what?" Mico's hardly winded, even though he was supposedly too sick to school a week ago.

"It's a food thing. About the geese."

Most of the real meat here is goose or duck. We harvest sustainably; the town gets a share before export. Gran says it's cleaner work than making nuclear batteries at the diamond plant; she rants, sometimes when she's drunk, about food being more virtuous than electricity.

Duck Sink makes feather and bone meal, makes goose fat and turnip-goose stew, organic pemmican and ...

... and?

This is why I only scored vermillion on my local resource quiz. The last item on every list always escapes me, like a skunk vanishing into the forest, leaving me in stink.

"Geese, geese, geese. Let's rename the village Goose Butt," Mico says.

"The vote's basically: do we want to give up another share of the protein stock and breast meat to Fort Saint John? If so, would we want to trade for real blueberries for six weeks each summer, or would we rather have rye bread twists?"

"I don't even know what rye bread is."

"Yeah, they'll tell us. There's gonna be a *tasting*."

He snorts. "Everyone will go for whatever's sweetest."

I shrug. It's my first vote, but if Mico doesn't think it's cool then I'm not going to show it. Luckily there's another hill then, and it's too much work, pedalling to the peak, for him to dampen my spirits further. As we crest it we see the longhouse, the polling stations where each community votes and markets and negotiates trade allocations. Long bundles of our goose feathers blow in the wind, strung from flagpoles. The kids from Diamond Collective, from the good side of town, are already there, circling the lot. Some of their bikes have smart tires.

"Maybe I'll just fail the stakeholder quiz."

"Mico!" I'm true shocked. "Fail?"

"You gotta pass to vote, right? Show you know the issues."

I think about tasting berries and twists of bread. I wonder if a hint of sweetness would be worth giving up the heavy fill of goose in your belly in February, that sense of being fed, well fed, when the snow's flying and the nights are long.

"C'mon," Mico says. "If we fail out of the stakeholder quiz, we can probably take those flashy bikes out for a spin while the others finish the unit."

As if in agreement, one of the Diamond kids does a spin, then pops up onto their back wheel and bounces, once, twice. Nobody yells at her not to damage the frame.

There's a long straightaway behind the school. I wonder how fast I could push a bike like that, if I pedalled hard.

Mico gives me his best shit-and-trouble grin.

Gran said that today I get to decide something for my little sister, for my cousin El. She says even if I go to Saskatoon when I'm grown, they all remain home, facing a plate that I made. That I decided on.

"We can race, Fezzi. You're crap at tests anyway, aren't you?"

Berries, bread, or goose.

"It's not that kind of test," I say, and then, before he can lean into the sales pitch: "And we can race now. I'll beat you to the lot!"

I stand up on my bike, then, and pedal for all I'm worth, picking up speed in spite of my dumb tires, chasing Kezia in her chair, chasing the future and all my classmates. Stealing a head start, and leaving Mico to decide if he's in or out as I fly downhill with my face bent to a wind of my own making, scenting for a future of skunk and summer blueberries.

ABOUT THE AUTHOR

Toronto author and editor L. X. Beckett frittered their youth working as an actor and theatre technician in Southern Alberta before deciding to make a shift into writing science fiction. Their first novella, "Freezing Rain, a Chance of Falling," appeared in the July/August issue of the *Magazine of Fantasy and Science Fiction* in 2018, and takes place in the same universe as their 2019 novel *Gamechanger*. Lex identifies as feminist, lesbian, genderqueer, married, and Slytherin. An insatiable consumer of mystery and crime fiction, as well as true crime narratives, they can be found on Twitter at @LXBeckett or at the Lexicon, lxbeckett.com.

ABOUT THE EDITOR

KATRINA Archer is the author of dark fantasy *The Tree of Souls* and YA fantasy *Untalented*, a *Library Journal* Indie Ebook Award Honorable Mention. A former software engineer, she lives on her sailboat in Vancouver, BC, Canada. Katrina has worked in aerospace, video games, and film, and is a freelance copy editor and publisher of climate change site *Little Blue Marble*. She can operate almost any vehicle that can't fly, doesn't believe in life without books or chocolate, and was once owned by a cat more famous in Germany than she is. Connect with her online at www.katrinaarcher.com.

For more great fiction and features about our changing climate, join us at

LittleBlueMarble.ca

Also available from *Little Blue Marble:*

Little Blue Marble 2017: Stories of Our Changing Climate

Little Blue Marble 2018: More Stories of Our Changing Climate

Little Blue Marble 2019: Climate in Crisis

LITTLE BLUE MARBLE
2020

GREENER FUTURES

An anthology of speculative climate fiction and poetry
by authors from around the world.

Fishing for ghosts. Saving the Agassiz Icefield.
A new North strong and sustainable.
Robot mermaids with lasers.
Teenage solar rogues. Activist archivists.
The Queen of the May and the protean Lord of the Sea,
struggling to cope with changes large and small.
A future West both weird and wild.
These greener futures hold all this and more.

ISBN 978-1-988293-10-3

9 781988 293103

Cover design by K. Archer

littlebluemarble.ca
ganachemedia.com